SACRIFICE

SACRIFICE

A Celtic Adventure

PHILIP FREEMAN

PEGASUS BOOKS
NEW YORK LONDON

SACRIFICE

Pegasus Books LLC
80 Broad Street, 5th Floor
New York, NY 10004

Copyright © 2015 Philip Freeman

First Pegasus Books edition October 2015

Interior design by Maria Fernandez

Ireland map courtesy of the author.

Library of Congress Cataloging-in-Publication Data is available.

ISBN: 978-1-60598-889-4

10 9 8 7 6 5 4 3 2 1

Printed in the United States of America
Distributed by W. W. Norton & Company

For Kenzie

IRELAND

SACRIFICE

Chapter One

N o, no, no! Deirdre, you don't add the wine until *after*
you stir in the fish sauce."

"Grandmother, I have been cooking this dish for
twenty years. I think I know by now when to add the sauce.
And besides, you're the one who taught me how to make it."

"Well, then I didn't do a very good job, because you're supposed to put the wine in last, or it will boil off and you'll lose
the flavor."

My grandmother and I were in her hut near Brigid's monastery cooking a special May Day dinner for Father Ailbe, Dari,
and two of Grandmother's druid friends. It was not going
well. Early that morning I had taken a loin of pork from her
smokehouse and simmered it in an iron pot with bay leaves,

peppercorns, celery, and a spoonful of honey. Grandmother had hovered over me the whole time, making sure I didn't cook the pork too quickly. After an hour, I took the pot off the hook over the fireplace and set it aside to cool. Meanwhile, my grandmother was making the dessert, a plum custard flavored with cumin and raisin wine.

"Ailbe and the rest will be here any minute. Deirdre, make yourself useful and fetch a jug of wine from the wellhouse. But be careful not to break it. This Gaulish pottery is so fragile, not like the solid Roman stuff from the old days."

"Grandmother, I'm not five years old anymore. I won't break the wine jar or ruin the dinner."

She waved me away as she stirred the custard. I stomped out the front door and went down the path to the small stone hut near the well. I grabbed a jar of wine from the back of the cool, damp building and made a point of banging it against the side of the door as I left. As much as I loved my grandmother and was grateful to her for raising me after my mother died, there were times when she made me want to scream.

"How's the dinner coming?"

I turned toward the familiar woman's voice and saw Dari and Father Ailbe coming up the path that stretched through the woods back to the monastery at Kildare. Dari was holding Father Ailbe's arm to steady him on the rocky path. She held a bundle of yellow buttercups in her other hand.

"A gift for your grandmother," she said. "I wish she would have let us bring some food to help with the dinner, but at least these should brighten the table."

Dari wore a typical bright smile on her face. I was always amazed that she managed to look so cheerful and that her long blond hair always seemed in place. My own dark red hair was frazzled and generally looked like I had just been caught in a windstorm.

"Dari, be glad you didn't bring anything to eat. Nothing would be good enough for that woman."

"Oh, having a little trouble around the cooking fire, are we?" she asked with a twinkle in her eye. She knew very well how my grandmother and I clashed in the kitchen.

"Don't get me started. I want this to be an enjoyable meal for all of us."

Father Ailbe stood next to her, waiting patiently. He had heard all my complaints before and knew they were a regular part of my visits home from the monastery. He had once been a tall man, but more than eighty years of life had left him slightly bent. Still, I was pleased to see him looking so well on this lovely spring day. I knew the winter had been hard on him, as it had on us all, but I could tell he had gained back some weight and that his color was much better. I reached out and gave him a big hug.

"Thank you, my dear, but what was that for?" he asked as I let go.

"No reason, Abba. I'm just happy to have you here today."

I had called him "Abba" since I was a little girl and couldn't pronounce his name properly. I took his other arm and walked to my grandmother's house with them. She was stirring the pudding as we came in.

"Ailbe, welcome, and you as well, Dari. Sorry the dinner is a little late. We've been having a bit of trouble with the main dish."

Before I could think of some witty comment, Father Ailbe spoke up.

"Aoife, you're so kind to invite us here today. I know what a busy time Beltaine is for you and the other members of the Order. Are you going to King Dúnlaing's festival tonight?"

"Yes, I'm lighting the sacred fire and helping with the sacrifices. You know you're invited as well. The king is always glad to see you."

"And I him, but it's a long walk to his farm and my knee has been bothering me today. My arthritis is acting up again."

"Well, you're the physician. You know that a brew of willow bark with a touch of clove will help with that."

"Yes, but like most doctors I'm a terrible patient. Please do give the king my regards."

"Aoife," said Dari, "I brought some fresh flowers for the table. May I put them in a vase with water?"

"Yes, of course, and thank you, my dear. It's so nice to have such a thoughtful young woman visit my home. Proper respect for one's elders is so rare nowadays. Would you like to help with the pork?"

Father Ailbe shook his head, urging me silently not to say anything.

There was a knock at the door. I opened it to find two elderly women standing in front of the hut. They wore the distinctive white tunics of druids under their cloaks and had slender golden torques about their necks. Their long gray hair was tied in braids down their backs.

"Cáma, Sinann, please come in," said my grandmother as she swept past me to greet them. "Deirdre, were you going to make them wait outside all day? Fetch some cups and pour everyone a glass of wine."

Both of the women were friends of Father Ailbe and greeted him warmly. Dari took their cloaks and placed them on my old bed near the door. Everyone sat down at the table, aside from my grandmother, who was still fussing with dinner. She laid the hot bread fresh from the hearth on the mantel to cool for slicing and placed a small jar of her special butter-and-honey relish on the table with a wooden spoon. She then sat with us and took a sip of the wine.

"Not bad," she said. "It was a gift from King Eógan after I used a vision to help him find one of his prize rams that had wandered into the hills."

"That man would lose his head if it wasn't attached to his neck," said Cáma. "He called on me last year to interpret a dream he had after three of his horses wandered off. He had some silly night vision about them being taken by dragons, but any fool could have told him they would be grazing on the summer grass near the Avoca River, which they were."

We all laughed as Dari refilled the cups.

"So, Sinann, how are the heavens looking lately?" asked my grandmother. "It was beautiful last night. You must have been up late gazing at the stars."

"Yes, indeed, the skies are rarely so clear. I was able to measure the angle of separation between the pole star and true north more accurately than ever before. I also found a new tailed star, very faint, just below the Great Bear's nose."

"A new tailed star, really?" asked Father Ailbe. "Do you think it will grow brighter?"

"Hard to say. These tailed stars—or comets as you Greeks call them," she said with a teasing glance at Father Ailbe, "usually fade away in a few days."

"Could it be an evil omen?" asked my grandmother.

"Possibly," said Sinann. "I don't put much stock in astromancy, but this star has a nasty red tinge to it. I'll be watching it to see what happens."

"Sinann, are you and Cáma going to the festival tonight?"

"Oh, yes, Ailbe, we're helping Aoife with the sacrifices. I thought Dúnlaing might have invited Finian to perform the rituals, but he can't stand the young man, no matter how skilled a sacrificer he is."

"I'm sorry," Dari said, "I don't know as much about the druids as I should, but do you mean that any druid can perform the job of any other druid? I thought there were different positions within the Order."

Although teaching comes naturally to the druids and we're always glad to share our knowledge, I was a little perturbed with Dari. I had tried to explain all this to her before, but she never showed any interest in learning about the druids from me.

"Yes, my child," Cáma answered, "there are many different roles within the Order, but we all receive the same extensive training in the foundations of druidic teachings. Any of us can, for example, officiate at ceremonies, offer sacrifices, or render judgments in legal cases. Just last week I performed a wedding and two funerals and settled a boundary dispute between some local farmers. But we each have our special areas of expertise that require years of extra study. I'm an interpreter of dreams and Sinann studies the workings of the heavens, while your friend Deirdre is a bard and her grandmother a seer. Still, while people come to me to understand their dreams, they could also go to Aoife, who would do a wonderful job."

"Oh, but not as well as you, my dear," protested my grandmother.

"And I was never good at visions like you, Aoife," Sinann said.

"But you're the best astronomer in Ireland," I said.

"Just as you're our most talented young bard," Cáma added.

"Ladies, please," Father Ailbe said as he raised his hand. "Let us agree that you're all wonderful at what you do. Now, is it just me, or is anyone else hungry?"

Everyone laughed, then Grandmother put the pork loin on a platter with garnishes while Dari and I set the table with plates and knives. We then brought the bread and pork to the table and all took our seats. Dinner smelled simply marvelous.

"Ailbe, would you like to ask a blessing on the meal?"

Grandmother normally wanted nothing to do with Christian rituals, especially after I became a nun, but she was a gracious host. I knew that Cáma and Sinann would have no objection to a Christian prayer since most druids are open to all aspects of the divine. Father Ailbe, for his part, had the greatest respect for Irish traditions and always urged understanding and harmony between the religions of our island.

"I would be honored, Aoife."

Father Ailbe bowed his head and made the sign of the cross on his chest, as did Dari and I, while the three druids sat in silence with their eyes closed and hands raised to the sky.

He began to pray.

"Master of the Universe, Creator of us all, grant us your grace—"

"Father Ailbe! Father Ailbe!"

A young girl was shouting in the distance. We could hear her running up the path from the monastery. We rushed out the door together and met her in the yard as she burst through the trees. It was Neala, a slender girl of about eight who was a student at our monastery. She was the fastest runner at Kildare and always beat the boys in the races we held at school contests. She was frantic as she ran to us and fell into Dari's arms.

"Neala, what's wrong?" Dari asked as we knelt beside her.

Her chest was heaving as she tried to breathe. Father Ailbe urged her to sit quietly and catch her breath, but the girl kept trying, unsuccessfully, to talk. At last she grabbed Father Ailbe's hand and began to pull him back down the road.

"Neala, child, what's wrong? Tell us," he said.

"Father—you—must—come—now," she managed at last.

"Why, Neala? What's happened? Is someone hurt?" he asked. She shook her head.

"No—not hurt—Sister Grainne—in bog."

"Sister Grainne is in a bog? That doesn't make sense. Does she need help?"

The poor girl burst into tears as Dari held her.

"No—she—has been—murdered."

Chapter Two

S ister Grainne was from one of the eastern clans of our tribe along the River Liffey, like many of the nuns at our monastery. She was a lovely, gentle woman about seventy years old and a devout Christian who lived as a solitary in a small hermitage just beyond the Red Hills northwest of the monastery. Like the dozen or so other solitaries associated with Brigid's church at Kildare, she practiced a quiet life of prayer and contemplation. She would come to the monastery about once a month for Sunday services and to bring us some of the excellent cheeses she made from the milk of her single dairy cow. Like most of the solitaries, she had no possessions of value in her small hut. I had known Grainne for years and couldn't believe anyone would want to hurt her.

When Neala had finally calmed down, she told us that a passing farmer had found Grainne's body in a bog next to her hermitage early that same morning. She appeared to have wounds from three crushing blows to the back of her head. The farmer had wrapped her in a blanket and gently loaded her into his cart. Her cow was still in her barn, lowing from a full udder, so the farmer milked it quickly, tied it to his cart, and came straight to the monastery. Sister Anna, our abbess, ordered the body taken to the infirmary and sent Neala to find Father Ailbe.

We left dinner on the table and rushed as fast as we could back to the monastery. Everyone went, including my grandmother, Cáma, and Sinann, none of whom could believe such a thing had happened at Kildare. Death from disease, hunger, and war was common enough in our land, but murder was a rare event. The hurried walk back to the monastery was hard on Father Ailbe, but he insisted that he could keep up with the rest of us. As we entered the gate, I saw a small crowd of monks and nuns gathered outside the infirmary, some praying, some weeping, but most just looking confused and frightened. Sister Anna met us at the door.

"Father Ailbe, we have placed the body on the table for you to examine. The farmer who brought her is waiting in the church if you wish to speak with him."

Sister Anna was the only member of the monastery who appeared unemotional in the face of this shocking event. She was the most stern and unbending person I had ever known, but also one of the most intelligent, and I knew she was deeply devoted to the people under her care. I also realized her self-control was dictated by the need for calm leadership in this moment of crisis.

"Let's leave the farmer there for now," said Father Ailbe. "I want to see the body first. Deirdre, I may need your assistance."

"Of course, Abba."

"I would like to be present as well," said Sister Anna.

"Certainly."

"Ailbe, may I come with you too?" asked my grandmother.

I wasn't surprised at this request. Grandmother had been Grainne's friend for many years. She would visit her hermitage whenever she passed that way, and Grainne was a frequent guest at her home as well.

"Yes, please join us," he said.

The four of us stooped to enter the infirmary door. It was a small round hut of woven branches joined tightly with clay and mud like most of the monastery buildings. And like our other buildings, it had an overhanging thatched roof and a warm central heath fire. A colorful curtain separated the examination room on the right of the hut from the beds for the sick and injured on the left, though there were no patients in residence at the moment. Father Ailbe always kept both rooms cozy and cheerful for the sake of those who came to him. He said a physician's first task was to put a patient at ease. Dried medicinal herbs were hanging from the wooden rafters, while the shelves on the walls were lined with jars of powders and potions. I knew that in chests out of sight were the less-agreeable tools of medicine, like a jagged-toothed bone saw for amputations and a set of finely sharpened steel knives for surgery. In the middle of the room was a large sturdy wooden table. On top of this table, surrounded by candles, lay the body of Sister Grainne.

She was curled up in a fetal position as she had been found, with a wool blanket draped over her body except for her head. Aside from the pallor of death, she looked as if she were sleeping, with a face as calm as I had ever seen. My grandmother softly placed her hand on Grainne's shoulder and whispered a prayer to the gods. There were tears in her eyes as she gazed at her friend. I placed my own hand on my grandmother's arm to steady her.

"Grandmother, can you see anything? Any image of who might have done this?"

My grandmother, as a druid seer, could often sense images from touching an object or a person.

"No. Murder is too evil an act to leave a clear impression. It clouds everything with darkness."

"Aoife, you don't need to stay if you don't want to," Father Ailbe said. "This may not be easy to watch."

My grandmother shook her head.

"No, I'll be all right. I don't want to leave her."

Father Ailbe asked me to light several more candles and place them along the sides of the table. Then he carefully pulled back the blanket to expose the body.

Grainne was wearing a homespun tunic of coarse wool that reached from high on her neck to just above her ankles and was tied around her waist with a cloth belt. Her well-worn leather sandals were still on her feet. Her body and clothes smelled strongly of dampness from the bog water, but there were no signs of decomposition.

Father Ailbe began his examination with her head as I took notes for him on a wax tablet. He was the very soul of compassion, but he conducted the autopsy with composed professionalism.

Grainne's mouth was closed and there were no bruises or contusions on her face. Her eyes were shut as if they had been closed gently after death. Her expression was peaceful and serene.

Moving behind her, we could see her white hair matted with blood.

"Three wounds to the top rear of the skull," observed Father Ailbe. "A heavy blunt instrument, probably some sort of iron pole or the back of an axe. The assailant struck the victim from above and behind, as if Grainne were lying on the ground. The wounds are deep enough to have fractured the skull in three places, but not severe enough to have caused immediate death. The edges of the wounds on the scalp show swelling, confirming that they were inflicted on a living body."

I shivered at the thought of someone doing this horrible deed to Grainne.

"Abba, how could she look so peaceful if she was struck by a heavy instrument while still alive?"

"I don't know, Deirdre. There is something very strange about this death."

He returned to the examination as I helped him position Grainne on her back. With a knife, he cut the high neck at the front of her robe down to the waist to expose the top of her body.

"No visible lacerations or bruises to the chest or upper abdomen. The arms are similarly undamaged. The hands show no wounds to suggest that she fought off the assailants or resisted any blows. Her lanyard and cross are missing."

He put his ear to her skin and thumped her chest several times with his hand.

"The lungs are dry. No water inhalation, so she didn't drown. She was dead before she went into the water."

He looked at her neck again and stopped.

"Abba, what's wrong?"

"Look at this," he said.

Sister Anna, my grandmother, and I all leaned in as he tilted back her head to expose her neck.

"Her leather lanyard and cross are still here, but they're sunk so deeply into her flesh that I didn't see them at first," he said.

Around our necks, all the sisters of holy Brigid wore a simple leather cord from which hung a small wooden cross. It was what marked us to the world as nuns.

"I can't even get my fingers underneath. Deirdre, hand me the small knife from the box."

I passed it to him and he carefully cut the leather, easing it and the cross out of her skin. He placed them on the table beside her.

"Someone has tied knots in the cord—three knots—all in front above the windpipe next to the cross. But the only way I can think to get the cord this tight would be twisting it with a stick from behind."

"You mean she was garroted?" Sister Anna asked.

"Yes, I believe so. When the stick on the lanyard was rotated, it would have exerted tremendous force on the windpipe, cutting off her air supply. Then with continued turning, it would act as a tourniquet to the jugular vein, finally snapping her spinal column if tightened far enough. The force of the cross against her flesh aided in the deed. It also left a deep mark in her neck, like a brand. Help me turn her on her side."

He probed deeply into the back of her neck with his fingers.

"Yes, her spinal column has been fractured just below the fourth cervical vertebra."

"But Abba, wouldn't it have taken a very strong man to do that? It would narrow down our list of suspects."

"No, unfortunately it doesn't help. Even a child could garrote someone effectively if that person was taken unaware or didn't resist. It was a favorite form of murder among the street gangs of Alexandria when I was young because it could be used with such deadly force by anyone."

Grandmother was shaking. I put my arm around her to comfort her. It must have been terrible to see her friend's body like this. But she pushed me away.

"No, Deirdre, you don't understand. Ailbe, please look closely at her neck above the right jugular vein."

He stared at her for a moment, then turned Grainne's head to the left and probed the skin beneath where the garrote had been.

"There's an incision here, deep and expertly done, directly into the jugular vein. There's some swelling around the wound, again indicating that Grainne was alive when this cut was made, at least at first. But this doesn't make sense!"

Father Ailbe looked both surprised and sickened, emotions I rarely saw on his face since he had been through so much in his long life.

"Abba, why doesn't it make sense?"

"Because it means someone struck three blows to her head to render her unconscious, then took her lanyard off, tied knots in it, put it back on her neck, and began to garrote her. But before the garrote was tightened very far, probably just enough to cut off her air supply, someone made an incision into her jugular. The result would have been a rapid emptying of her entire blood supply before the assailant finished tightening the garrote."

Grandmother looked as white as a sheet. She sat down in a chair next to the table.

"Aoife, how did you know?" asked Sister Anna.

Grandmother didn't answer. I started to feel queasy myself as I realized what she suspected.

Father Ailbe completed his examination of the body. He said the time of death was hard to determine with certainty, but since Grainne had visited the monastery only a week earlier, we knew she had been murdered within the last seven days.

When Father Ailbe was finished, he sat beside my grandmother and held her hand.

"Aoife, what is it? How did you know about the wound to her neck?"

My grandmother shook her head before she spoke.

"Ailbe, I'm sorry to ask you to do this, but would you examine the contents of her stomach?"

"Is that really necessary?" asked Sister Anna. "I would prefer not to do any more damage to this poor woman's body."

"Please, Anna," said my grandmother. "It's important."

Father Ailbe rose silently and went back to the table. He took a larger knife from the box, along with a pair of clamps.

"Deirdre, I'm going to need your help."

I had butchered many animals in my life and had helped Father Ailbe perform surgery on numerous patients. I was not a squeamish person, but I had never been part of an autopsy like this. I forced myself to calm down and tried very hard not to throw up.

Father Ailbe cut deeply into Grainne's abdomen while I pulled the flesh away to expose her stomach. He then made an incision and told me to hold back the tissue with the clamps. As far as I could tell, her stomach was empty. Father Ailbe probed inside with his fingers, then bent over her body. He sniffed the air around her, then placed his nose directly above the incision.

"There's a strange, bitter odor in her stomach. Aoife, please come and tell me what you think."

I had never seen Grandmother look so afraid as she approached the table. She held on to the side as she bent over the cavity. It was only a moment later that her knees gave way and she slumped to the floor. I eased her up and helped her back into the chair.

"Grandmother, is it what I think?"

"Yes. It's mistletoe."

"No—dear God in heaven," I whispered.

Sister Anna marched quickly across the room and stood in front of us.

"Aoife, what is going on? One of the sisters of my monastery has been murdered, and you two seem to know something about it I don't. Tell me now."

Grandmother stood and faced the abbess as I held her. Her voice was barely audible.

"Anna, she wasn't murdered."

"What do you mean she wasn't murdered? It hardly seems like suicide."

"No, you don't understand," Grandmother said. "The drink of mistletoe, the three blows to the head to stun her, the garrote with three knots, the draining of her blood, her placement in water after she was dead. It was all done according to the ritual."

"What ritual? What are you talking about?"

She took a deep breath before answering.

"Grainne wasn't murdered. She was sacrificed."

Chapter Three

Sister Anna covered Grainne's body with the blanket and told us to say nothing as we left the infirmary together. All the monks and nuns of Kildare, along with many of the monastery widows and our neighbors, were gathered outside the hut waiting for news, but Sister Anna told the crowd that we didn't know anything yet. She asked Dari to stay with the body and allow no one inside while the four of us went to the church to talk with the man who had found Grainne.

He was standing near the altar next to the chest holding holy Brigid's bones. We spoke to him briefly, but it was clear that he had little to add to what we already knew. He had been passing by the bog early that morning on a frequently traveled road leading to Kildare. He had seen the body in shallow water surrounded by reeds and pulled it out. He put Grainne's corpse in his cart without disturbing it in any way and brought her immediately to the monastery, along with her cow. He was an honest young man who was well known to us, and there was no reason to suspect him of foul play.

Sister Anna thanked and dismissed him, then led us to the small stone hut that served as her office. Father Ailbe and my grandmother sat in the two chairs in front of her desk, while I stood behind them. Sister Anna closed the window shutters, then bolted the door.

"Now," she said, "tell me exactly what you meant when you said Sister Grainne was sacrificed."

My grandmother took a moment to collect herself before she began.

"Anna, the sacrifice of animals to the gods is an important part of druidic practice, just as in the old religion of the Romans. Among the druids, offerings are a way to preserve the balance of nature by giving something precious to the divine forces who control our world in exchange for their blessings on the land and in our lives. A farmer sacrifices a goat in exchange for a good harvest, a mother sacrifices a chicken for the healing of her child—"

"Yes, Aoife, I understand the concept, but Grainne was not a goat or chicken."

"No, of course not. According to the teachings of the druids, the more precious a sacrifice offered to the gods, the more powerful the result. There is nothing more precious than human life. Centuries ago in Ireland, on rare and special occasions, the druids would sacrifice a living man or woman. Sometimes these were volunteers who acted from religious devotion, even druids and kings, and sometimes they were criminals condemned to die for offenses they had committed. Farmers still find the bodies of these victims on occasion when they dig for turf or drain a bog. But it has been hundreds of years since the last human sacrifice was performed on this island. Long ago, the Irish druids accepted the doctrine that properly honoring the gods does not require such extreme measures."

"And yet," said Father Ailbe, "Grainne lies on a table in our infirmary, dead not more than a week."

"Yes, and it was most certainly a deliberate sacrifice according to the ancient druidic ritual."

"How do you know that for certain?" asked Sister Anna.

"Because of the manner of her death, as well as its timing. Three is a sacred number among us, just as with your Christian threesome of father, son, and . . . what's the last one?"

"The Holy Spirit," answered Father Ailbe.

"Yes. We have triple deities as well. But it's not just in regard to gods that the number three is special. A sacred act progressing in thirds yielding a whole signifies completeness. Grainne was struck with a blunt instrument on the back of the head three times, but not in a way that would kill her outright. It was important that her blood still be flowing for the rest of the ritual."

"So being struck three times to the head wasn't the end," said Sister Anna.

"No, that was just the beginning, the first act of the sacrifice done with three strokes, sacred number within sacred number."

"What was the second act?"

"Strangulation with the garrote. Three knots instead of three strokes, but it had to be done very carefully. Only someone who was trained as a druid would know the importance and technique of crushing the windpipe at the beginning without cutting off the blood supply."

"But you said she was deliberately bled out in the middle of the garroting."

"Yes, the incision to the jugular vein had to be done with the greatest care by an expert to. . . . Anna, the next part of this is not pleasant."

"Aoife, one of my nuns has been killed. No part of this is pleasant to me."

"Of course. Grainne's head would have been forced down so that it was lower than the rest of her body, to collect her blood as it quickly drained from her. Sometimes victims were hung upside down by their feet to do this, but there was no evidence of ropes around her ankles, was there, Ailbe?"

"No."

"Well, it would work either way. After the blood was collected in a bowl, it would have been offered to the god."

"Which god?" asked Sister Anna.

"Bel, the one honored on this holy day of Beltaine. He is the god of summer and fertility of the land at the start of the season, the divine bearer of male seed to the feminine earth."

"What happened after Grainne's blood was drained?"

"The sacrificer would have tightened the garrote the rest of the way to seal off any remaining blood flow and guarantee death with the crushing of the neck."

"Was there any significance to the use of her lanyard with the cross as a garrote?" asked Father Ailbe.

"Not that I can think of. Any kind of cord or wire could be used, as long as it was very strong. I suppose the killer had a sense of irony using a Christian object for a druidic execution."

"Irony?" Sister Anna stood up. "Do you think this is in any way amusing, Aoife?"

Grandmother rose from her chair and faced Sister Anna.

"Don't twist my words. Grainne was my friend!"

"Please," I said as I moved between them. "Grandmother, Sister Anna, this is a terrible time for all of us. We have to work together if we're going to find the killer."

Both women eased back into their chairs. My grandmother continued.

"Draining the blood is not the third element of the sacrifice, it is simply a way of gathering the essence of life as an offering to the god. The third act was the drowning in the bog."

"But she was already dead, wasn't she?" asked Sister Anna.

"Most certainly," said Father Ailbe.

"Yes," said my grandmother. "The drowning is symbolic. It is the final element in what druids call the Triple Death."

"How does the mistletoe fit into the ritual?" asked Father Ailbe. "I think I can guess, but I would like to hear about it from you, Aoife."

"Mistletoe is a plant sacred to the druids. It's an ancient tradition that goes back to the beginnings of the Order in Britain. It grows on oaks, our most holy tree, and its berries have many medicinal uses, for both animals and people."

"But," interjected Father Ailbe, "it is extremely difficult to use safely. The extraction and preparation of the juice from the berries has to be done very carefully. Too little of it will make a patient violently ill, too much will cause an immediate cessation of breathing and heartbeat."

"That's why only a trained druid can use it properly in a sacrifice," Grandmother said. "The preparation and exact amount is critical."

"For what?" asked Sister Anna.

"To render the victim unconscious," I said.

"Yes," said my grandmother. "The druids of ancient times taught that it was important for the victim not to suffer. In fact it was an integral factor in the sacrifice. If the person offered to the gods in most sacrifices experienced pain or terror, it negated the ritual. Indeed, it became a curse on the druid who performed the rite. I thank the gods that at least Grainne didn't die in agony and fear."

"But," I added, "the amount of mistletoe could not be enough to bring about death by itself. The victim needed to be alive for the rest of the ritual."

"So that's why you wanted to examine the contents of Sister Grainne's stomach," Sister Anna said. "To see if she had consumed mistletoe."

"Yes," said my grandmother. "The odor of mistletoe prepared by a druid is unmistakable."

"But how would the murderer have persuaded Grainne to ingest it?" asked Father Ailbe. "I presume it was put into a drink of some kind to cover the bitter taste?"

"That would be the normal way," said my grandmother. "And it was important that the victim take the cup willingly. Even in centuries past when criminals were sacrificed, it was crucial that they accept the drink freely."

"How would a murderer do that with Sister Grainne?" asked the abbess. "Could he have intimidated her in some way, perhaps threatening to harm someone or something she cared about?"

"That is possible," Grandmother said. "He could also have tricked her somehow, though that was never done in the old days."

Sister Anna got up and paced behind her desk as she considered this information; then she spoke.

"You keep talking about how these sacrifices were done in the past, centuries ago, but if they are obsolete how would any druid today know what to do? How would he have learned the method of garroting and draining blood or the exact preparation of mistletoe to bring about unconsciousness in a victim but not death?"

My grandmother looked uncomfortable, but finally spoke.

"Anna, the teachings of the druids are secret. I can't go into any more detail with you than I already have. But I can tell you that druids today still learn the old ways, even though we would never practice them now."

Sister Anna placed her hands on her desk and looked at my grandmother in disbelief. Even Father Ailbe seemed surprised.

"Do you mean to tell me," she asked, "that not five miles from here at the druidic school, you are teaching young members of the Order how to perform human sacrifices?"

I answered for her.

"Sister Anna, you must understand, these rituals are part of our heritage, our sacred traditions. We study them in the way the Jews still study the details of animal sacrifice, even though the Romans destroyed their temple in Jerusalem almost five hundred years ago."

"The key difference, Sister Deirdre, is that the Jews never sacrificed human beings. Are you saying that when you were a child, I allowed you to leave your classes early here at the monastery so that you could walk down the road and learn the best way to slaughter someone on a bloody altar?"

My grandmother stood up and faced Sister Anna again.

"Leave her alone, Anna. You don't understand what you're talking about. The ancient rituals of human sacrifice are only a fraction of what Deirdre or any other young druid learns. And it was never meant to be instruction in performing the deed. It is part of a much larger appreciation of our traditions."

"Well, Aoife," said Sister Anna, "you and your precious traditions have taught someone how to kill one of my nuns in the most gruesome way I could imagine!"

Grandmother started toward the abbess, but both Father Ailbe and I held her back.

"How dare you!" hissed my grandmother.

"Get out, Aoife!" shouted Anna. "Go back to your sacred groves and brew up some way to bring Grainne back to life if you can."

Grandmother stormed out of the hut, slamming the door behind her. There was a long, painful silence before Father Ailbe spoke.

"Deirdre, can you tell us anything else that might help us find the killer? Any details about the killing that might point to some particular druid or group within the Order?"

I shook my head.

"I'm sorry, Abba, but Grandmother told you as much as anyone inside the Order can reveal to non-druids. I'll do anything I can to help you find the killer, but I can't betray the secret doctrines of the druids, not even to you."

"Sister Deirdre," said the abbess. "When you stood here a few months ago after the theft of holy Brigid's bones, I warned you that I would not accept your disobedience again. Do you remember?"

"Yes, Sister Anna," I said with my head bowed.

"And yet here you are again keeping secrets, refusing to answer questions that involve the death of a sister of yours in the fellowship of Brigid, someone who was murdered in the most terrible manner."

I remained standing in silence.

"I must go now," she said, "first to tell the members of the monastery that Grainne was murdered by one of your druids, then to send word of this deed to King Dúnlaing. But I want you to consider where your loyalties lie. No man or woman can serve two masters. I have indulged you these past three years as you have tried to be both a druid and a Christian nun, but you must choose which side you are on."

She left the hut and walked to the church to ring the bell for assembly. I remained standing in front of her desk, with Father Ailbe beside me.

"Abba, we should go to the church with the others. I want to say a prayer to Brigid to watch over the soul of Grainne."

We walked out the door and made our way across the monastery yard with the other brothers and sisters. The spring day that had started out so bright and beautiful had turned dark and cold, with rain pouring down from the heavens.

Chapter Four

T he shock of the sisters and brothers after the abbess made her announcement in the church that evening was heartbreaking. There were gasps of disbelief at first, then moaning and weeping, and finally looks of anger among a few as they turned to stare at me.

I wasn't hungry and didn't want to talk to anyone at dinner, so I remained in the church after the others left so that I could pray and think. After perhaps half an hour, Sister Macha entered and cleared her throat.

"Deirdre, I'm sorry to bother you, but Sister Anna would like to see you in her office right away."

"All right. How are you doing, Macha? I'm sorry I talked you into leaving Armagh and coming here to go through this terrible time with us."

Macha had returned with Dari and me when we had visited the monastery of Armagh in Ulster a few months earlier. The nuns there were treated almost like slaves, laboring at menial tasks for the abbot and denied any kind of education. Macha was already making great progress in learning to read and write.

She managed a weak laugh.

"Don't be sorry at all, Deirdre. The last few months here at Kildare have been the best of my life. There's plenty of sorrow wherever you go on this island."

I left the church and went across the monastery yard to the cold stone hut of Sister Anna. It was small, but served as both her office and sleeping quarters. I knocked on the door.

"Come in."

Sister Anna was sitting at her desk, finishing a letter. I stood in front of her and waited in silence until she was done. She wrote with her left hand, her right arm hanging useless at her side as always. The deep scars on the right side of her face were illuminated by the light of the oil lamp on her desk.

"This letter is to King Dúnlaing," she said at last. "I'm sending it to him by messenger this evening. I called you here because I need your help, Sister Deirdre. I'm sure the king will conduct his own inquiry into the death of Sister Grainne, but I'm not prepared to wait for him, nor would I fully trust his results. Kings often care more about politics than discovering the truth. I therefore have a task for you. You recovered the stolen bones of Brigid last winter after I put you in charge of that investigation. Your success in that venture recommends you for another. In addition, you are uniquely suited for this new commission since you are, as you so often remind me, a druid. I want you to investigate Grainne's death yourself, using your knowledge of the Order. But I need to know first that I can trust you.

Will you place the needs of this monastery above all other considerations?"

I had been expecting this and on the way over from the church had been considering what I should say to the abbess. I took a deep breath.

"Sister Anna, I am both a druid and a nun. I see no conflict between the two. I worship Christ and serve the church while respecting the ancient traditions of my people as a bard. I am honored that you have asked me to find the killer of Sister Grainne. I will use all my skills and training as a druid to find the man who committed this vicious act. It is as much an offense to the druids as it is to any Christian. I believe I can do this without betraying the vows I took to either the Order or to this monastery. But please do not ask me to reveal to you or anyone outside the Order any secrets of the druids."

She tapped her stylus on her desk several times before she spoke.

"You put me in a difficult position, Sister Deirdre. I need your expertise to solve this crime, but I also need your obedience. As you may have noticed through the years, I do not like or trust the druids. I have always maintained good relations with the Order for the sake of this monastery, but I am not like Brigid—or you. I do not believe we can all work together for a common spiritual goal. We share many values with the druids, but in the end our ways are not compatible. There is either one God or many, one path to salvation or not, one life followed by judgment or endless reincarnations as the druids teach. Christ either died to redeem the whole world or he didn't. I confess that my feelings about the Order are colored by my own experiences, but I cannot change who I am."

I knew it was not my place to ask Sister Anna about her personal life. She was a deeply private woman who never talked about her past. She was from Britain—several of the sisters were, but they had all left their homeland of their own free will to come to Ireland and follow Brigid's path. Still, I had to know.

"Sister, what do you mean when you say your feelings are colored by your own experiences? Why do you feel this way about the druids?"

The abbess scowled at me.

"That, Sister Deirdre, is none of your business."

"Yes, Sister Anna, you're right, of course. It's just that my grandmother once told me that you know more about the ways of the druids than most."

"What did she tell you?" she asked angrily. "How would she know anything about my past?"

"She wouldn't tell me anything more. I had the feeling she herself didn't know much, perhaps just bits of a story she had heard long ago from some other druids."

Sister Anna looked at me hard, with anger and pain in her eyes.

"Do you really want to know, Sister Deirdre? Perhaps I should tell you, just so you can learn the truth about the druids you so honor and protect."

She rose from her chair and stared out the window for a long time. I heard a dog barking somewhere in the distance. At last she spoke, her voice cold and empty, not even turning toward me, as if she were talking to the growing darkness.

"I was born on a small farm on the western coast of Britain near the old Roman town of Luguvalium. My baptismal name was Anna, though my father always called me Blodeuyn, which in my language means 'flower.' He was a giant of a man, but he was always gentle with me. My mother was the disciplinarian in the family. She worked hard to keep us alive every winter when the north wind blew down from the land of the Picts. I had two sisters and an older brother who helped on the farm, just as I did. I was the youngest. My most important job was to feed the chickens and collect their eggs each morning. We never had much, but we were happy.

"The Irish raiders came in the spring, just after the seed was in the ground. They slipped into our farm quietly at night and surrounded the place before we realized what was happening. Somehow my father awoke and knew something was terribly wrong. He roused everyone and told us to stay hidden while he and my brother took the two rusty swords we kept in the house and rushed out into the yard. There were perhaps a dozen pirates waiting. They laughed at my father and brother standing there determined to protect us from so many of them. They changed their minds when my father skewered one through the heart with his sword and threw another against our low stone wall, breaking his back. The remaining men rushed my father and brother, hacking them both to pieces as we watched from the window.

"The men burst through the door of the hut and grabbed my mother, my sisters, and me and tied us with ropes. After they had stolen what little of value they could find, they raped us, taking turns while the others ate what food we had. I was ten years old. The last thing I remember before they marched us to their boat was the sight of my chickens bound by the feet and hanging over the shoulders of one of the raiders as he carried them away.

"I barely remember the miserable trip across the Eastern Sea and I don't know where we landed, though it must have been somewhere on the coast of Ulster. We were herded into a pen with other female captives to wait for the auction that would come the next day. I clung to my mother and sisters, but they were in no shape to provide me comfort. The raiders had been particularly hard on my mother, probably because she was older and wouldn't bring them much of a profit. She had grown sick on the voyage from Britain and burned with a fever. By morning she was dead.

"I was sold to a druid who pulled me away from my sisters as I begged them not to let me go. I never saw them again and don't know if they are still alive somewhere on this island. I hope for their sake they are not. I will spare you the details of my captivity since you know how slaves are treated in your homeland. They are the lowest form of life, a class beneath contempt, given no more respect than a dog, often less. I did as I was told or was beaten. I was frequently beaten anyway. I learned to keep quiet and tried to be invisible as I performed the most menial chores around the farm, often grinding grain on the quern for hours until my hands were raw. They even took away my name, calling me only *cumal*, which I thought was a name itself until I learned it was just the Irish word for a female slave.

"My master was a respected member of the Order. He frequently entertained high-ranking guests at his farm. I was a pretty girl then, so he often gave me to his visitors—most of them druids—as entertainment for the night. Over the next ten years, I was pregnant several times but thankfully never carried a child to term. Why would I have wished a living soul to be born into such a life? I prayed at first to God to free me as he had freed the Israelites from captivity in the land of Egypt, but there was no escape. Even if I could have fled, I would have been an *élúdach*, a runaway slave. Where could I have gone? According to your laws, even a king could not help me if he found me on the road, not that he would have wished to in any case.

"One autumn, my master took me with him when he officiated at a religious ceremony not far from here. He used me on such trips to cook his meals and to provide 'portable recreation,' as he called it. On the road he met a druid friend of his, and the two sat down to have a drink of honeyed wine. His friend kept looking at me in a way with which I was all too familiar and soon asked if he might have a few minutes with me. My master was glad to oblige and told me to take off my clothes and accommodate him. I don't know why, but something in me snapped at that moment. I shouted that I would rather sleep with one of his stinking pigs than give myself to another of his friends. He rose up red-faced and angrier than I had ever seen him. Not only had I dared to disobey his command, but I had shamed him in front of his companion. He grabbed me and began to hit me with his fists, then took an iron shovel from the back of the cart, beating me on my arm and face and breaking both my legs. When I fell to the ground, he kicked me again and again. I don't remember anything after that until I woke up hours later in a ditch beside the road. My master had left me for dead. As I lay in the mud, I prayed that God would let me die. A farmer and his family passed by in their wagon, as did a group of druids, hurrying to some sacrifice, no doubt. No one gave me a second glance.

"Then as the sun was setting and the cold was beginning to creep up my limbs, a sure sign of the end, a small woman appeared, wearing a strange hat. I thought she must be an angel come to take me to heaven, but she dragged me from the ditch into the dry grass and wrapped me in her cloak while she built a fire. She bathed my wounds and tried to feed me some broth, but I was only strong enough to take a little water. She lay beside me all through the night, sharing her warmth and keeping me alive.

"I don't remember how I got here, but two days later I woke up in this monastery with the same small woman at my bedside. It was Brigid, who continued to care for me with the help of the handful of other sisters she had gathered in those early days. It took months of nursing, but eventually I was able to walk again. My druid master never tried to find me, since he assumed I was dead, though I doubt he would have wanted me back in any case with these scars on my face and my useless arm. I stayed here with Brigid and have thanked God every day for the kindness she showed me when no one else cared."

Tears ran down my face as she finished. She glanced at me, then turned away.

"Don't look so shocked, Sister Deirdre. My story has been repeated many times on your island. Even Patrick was a slave among your people, though against all odds he escaped and made it home. In Britain, slaves can at least work hard and buy their freedom, but according to your druids such an act would offend the gods, causing the cows of the land to be barren and the fields to yield no fruit. So yes, my child, sinner that I am, I do hate the druids and all they represent. Your precious Order ruined my life. I was a flower once, but now I am only a shadow of that happy girl."

She continued to stare out the window.

"You may keep your druid secrets for now, Sister Deirdre," she said at last. "Begin your investigation. But if I believe you are withholding any information from me that will help us find the killer of one of my nuns, I will expel you from this monastery forever."

Chapter Five

I couldn't face anyone else that evening, so I left Sister Anna's office and went immediately to the small fire temple surrounded by a tall hedge on the far side of the church.

We all called it the fire temple, even though it was formally known as the Oratory of Holy Brigid. The monastery had been founded fifty years earlier as a religious community for women and men to live out the Gospel together by serving others. But long before Kildare was a church, it had been a sacred place of gathering for the women who served an ancient Irish goddess, also named Brigid, who watched over the special concerns of women. The priestesses of the goddess kept a perpetual fire burning in her honor at this same stone temple, much as the Vestal Virgins once did at their sanctuary in the Roman Forum before a Christian emperor extinguished it. By the time our Brigid arrived at Kildare, there was only one aged druid priestess left, who tended the sacred fire every night. Brigid promised her that the fire of the goddess would never go out if the sisters of Kildare were allowed to build their monastery there. The priestess agreed and left the fire temple in the care of Brigid, who kept her word. Though some of the bishops of Ireland had sought to extinguish the flame as a pagan abomination, Brigid proclaimed that the fire would now honor Christ as the light of the world. When she was still alive, I once asked her if she really believed this. She pulled me close and whispered that it never hurt to have a goddess on your side.

The nuns all took turns in the fire temple, for no man was ever allowed to enter that holy place. I was glad that it happened to be my night to tend the flame. I spread my blanket on the warm ground next to the fire and placed two logs from the woodpile into the hearth at the center. I loved the peace and quiet of the fire temple. It was a wonderful place to think without being disturbed. Of course, there was the night two years ago when a man burst in, shouting that he had leaped over the holy hedge while I was tending the flames, and he proceeded to blow on the fire so hard that I was afraid it might go out. It was old Finbar, a poor fellow lame in one foot who had lost his mind some time before and had come to live with us at the monastery. I finally calmed him down and got him back into bed, but the story later spread that he had been driven mad and made a cripple because he, as a man, had dared to enter the sacred precinct of the fire guarded by women.

But the night after my conversation with Sister Anna, I wasn't expecting any guests. I stirred the embers and thought about the dark events of the day.

Why would anyone, especially a druid, want to kill a kind and gentle woman like Grainne? Our people had never persecuted followers of Christ. Any missionary coming to our island hoping to become a martyr was disappointed. At worst, they would encounter polite indifference from the local people—more likely an invitation to dinner from a friendly druid who wanted to discuss the larger questions of spirituality. One disappointed zealot told me it was impossible to convert a people who were always finding points of agreement between their faith and yours.

But there was no doubt that the murderer was a druid. There was simply no one else who would have the knowledge needed to sacrifice a victim in the way Grainne had been killed. And no druid would ever divulge secret teachings to someone who was not a member of the Order, even under the most extraordinary circumstances. I knew several druids who had become devout Christians and even priests, but they would never discuss the sacred doctrines they had learned with those who had not been initiated.

I heard footsteps approaching the temple from beyond the hedge and then a knock on the wooden door. I was tempted not to answer it, but I knew who it would be. She was the one person I didn't mind talking to at that moment.

"Dari, come in. The door isn't latched."

She entered carrying a blanket and spread it on the dirt floor of the hut beside me. She also pulled a small jug of beer and a loaf of bread from her satchel and placed them in front of us. I wasn't hungry, but it was thoughtful of her. She put her arm around me, giving me a tight hug. I reached out and squeezed her hand in return.

We sat in silence for a few minutes. I knew she was going to let me speak first.

"Dari, I don't understand how this could have happened. Grainne was one of the most caring and thoughtful people I've ever known. Do you remember that night a couple of years ago when we stayed at her hermitage on the way back to Kildare? She gave us the last of her wine and insisted we sleep on her bed while she spread out a mat on the floor for herself. And she was funny, too. I still remember the joke she told last Easter about the goose who went to visit the two swans."

Dari laughed.

"I remember too. She was one of my favorite people in the world. She was the first person to welcome me when I came to the monastery from Ulster, just before I met you. She told me that everything was going to be all right after all the hard times I had been through. And she was right."

Dari began to cry.

"Deirdre, why would anyone kill her? She had no enemies. She had nothing worth stealing except a cow, and the murderer left that behind. And the way she was killed. Why would someone do such terrible things to her?"

"I know, Dari, believe me, I know. It doesn't make any sense. Even in ancient times, no druid would seek out an innocent old woman for a sacrifice. It's a blasphemy against everything the druids held—and hold—dear."

I saw a hedgehog peek its head through the door to the temple. They were strange little creatures with brown spikes covering their bodies except for their undersides and noses. This one lived in a hole by our barn. He had smelled our food and was trying to decide if it was something he might like. I tore off a piece of bread and tossed it to him. He sniffed it, looked at me as if to ask if that was all I was offering, then took it back into his den.

"How are the sisters back in the sleeping hut holding up?"

"No one is sleeping, as far as I could tell. Some were still crying when I left, some were gathered by the fire sharing stories about Grainne, and a couple were sitting on their cots just staring at the walls. Kevin moved her body from the infirmary to the church after you left. Sister Anna and some of the elderly nuns who knew her best are holding a vigil there. Father Ailbe is with them."

"I'm such a coward, hiding here. I should be there too."

"It's your turn in the fire temple. I'll take your place here if you want, but everyone understands. They also know how difficult this is for you. No one blames you because you're a druid."

"You always see the best in everyone, Dari. They may not blame me directly for Grainne's death, but I saw the way some of them looked at me in the church, especially Eithne."

Sister Eithne had been my nemesis since my first day as a child at the monastery school.

"Eithne has always looked at you like that. She'd blame you if the sky fell down on her head. As for the others, I think they're just frightened. It all happened so suddenly. They don't know what they're mad at or who to blame. You're the resident druid at our little monastery, so naturally they look at you suspiciously. It won't last."

Dari pulled her blond hair back behind her neck and tied it with a ribbon from her pocket. She was the same age as me, but she always managed to look younger than her thirty years. My grandmother once said she had the spirit of a woodlark and the courage of a she-wolf protecting her cubs.

"It doesn't really matter if some of them are mad at me, Dari. The problem is finding out who killed Grainne and finding out quickly. King Dúnlaing is going to be outraged by this brutal murder and see it as a blatant attack on his sovereignty. This is not some family revenge killing or an isolated raid by outlaws. It was cold and calculated and meant to strike fear into the hearts of us all. The king knows that a ruler who can't protect his own people is seen as weak in the eyes of everyone. Word of this killing will spread across Ireland, and other kings may try to take advantage of it. The last thing we need now is a war with another tribe. We're too weak after the years of fighting with the Uí Néill. We need time to heal."

"I hadn't thought of that. Honestly, I hadn't thought of anything except how much I'm going to miss Grainne."

"I know, Dari. It's just that I was born into the nobility of this island and can't help but know how they think. As much as some of them may genuinely grieve at the death of Grainne, they'll all consider how this might change the game of power they play. Who gets weaker, who gets stronger, what opportunities does this open—you can bet they're already talking about it at Dúnlaing's court. By next week, they'll be debating it from Munster to Ulster."

"Deirdre, I don't know about the politics of these things, but I've met a number of druids in my life, especially since you and I have become friends and I've gotten to know your grandmother. I know you can't talk about druid secrets, but what possible reason would a member of the Order have for killing Grainne?"

"That's just it, Dari. It doesn't make any sense. This kind of sacrifice hasn't been done for centuries. Even then, it was a rare event that was carefully debated by the whole druid community before being carried out, never an isolated action done by a lone druid or even a small group. And such a sacrifice was always meant to bring balance to the land. I'm afraid that Grainne's death is going to do just the opposite and throw everything into chaos."

Dari stared at the fire for a while, then yawned and stretched out her arms.

"Well, I for one would like to put this day behind me and begin again tomorrow. Why don't you throw a couple more logs on the fire to keep us both warm tonight."

"You don't have to stay if you don't want to. I'll be fine alone."

She smiled and stretched out on her blanket next to me. She was asleep almost as soon as her head touched the ground. I pulled her cloak over her and put more logs on the fire. Then I took my harp from its case and softly plucked the strings as I began to sing:

> *Where is God on a night such as this?*
> *Where is the mercy of Christ, the love of Mary,*
>   *the watching eyes of Brigid the fair?*
> *Where is Grainne, the gentle woman of Leinster,*
>   *who was a light in this dark, cold world?*
> *Dear Jesus, let her leap like a lamb*
>   *freed from its ropes as she enters the gates*
>   *of your kingdom on high,*
>   *never to know suffering again.*
> *And remember your children left here without her.*

I put away the harp and curled up beside Dari, tucking my cloak around her as well. I lay awake for a long time, watching the gentle dance of the flames in the fire.

Chapter Six

Dari and I were up early the next day for morning prayers in the church. I placed more logs on the hearth and banked the fire so it would burn until evening, when another sister would come and spend the night in the temple. We gathered our bedding to take back to the nuns' sleeping quarters before the service. I couldn't hide anymore. It was time to face whatever lay ahead.

"Did you sleep at all last night?" Dari asked as we walked through the muddy monastery yard. It had rained hard in the early morning hours, and the muck was even worse than usual.

"Not much. Maybe tonight will be better. Are you still holding classes this morning?"

Dari was the teacher of the youngest children at the monastery school.

"Oh, yes. The children are scared and confused, of course, but it's important that we go on as always. Little ones need consistency in their lives."

"Don't we all? I'm actually looking forward to getting back to work in the barn today. While I'm figuring out how to investigate this murder, I'm going to clean out the cattle stalls and patch up the fence on the far side of the pig pen. I'm not going to bother bathing until tonight."

I saw that Dari was no longer beside me but a few steps behind, staring into the distance.

"Deirdre, what is that?"

She was pointing to a tree trunk about a quarter of a mile away on a low rise south of the monastery. It was an ancient oak that had been struck by lightning a few years ago. The tree was dead, but the scarred remains of the bare trunk still rose like a blackened stake hammered into the ground by some angry god.

There were crows circling the tree. On the top fork of the trunk was some object I couldn't make out at that distance.

"I'm not sure, Dari. Maybe an animal? Hunters sometimes tie a deer to the tree to gut the carcass."

"I don't think so." Her eyes had always been better than mine. "Whatever's on top looks yellowish, like golden hair."

We dropped our blankets and began to run.

Brother Kevin must have seen it at the same time we did, since we all arrived at the tree together. For a moment the three of us just stared, trying to understand what we saw in front of us. Then Dari fell to the ground and threw up.

The naked body of a young woman was tied with thick ropes to the broken trunk of the tree. A crow that had been perched on her right shoulder had flown away when we came near.

Signs and emblems, all of which I knew were sacred druid symbols, had been carved into the flesh around her breasts with a knife. But there was no head on the body.

On the sharp point at the top of the tree, higher than I could reach, was the missing head of the woman, fixed as if on a pike. The golden blond hair was blowing in the wind, wrapping itself thickly around her face.

Others from the monastery were running to the tree now, including Sister Anna, who came and stood with us. I could also see Father Ailbe coming down the path as fast as he could.

The abbess took in the scene in a moment and made the sign of the cross on her chest.

"Sister Deirdre, how long have you been here?" she asked.

"I just arrived, along with Dari and Kevin. We were spending the night in the fire temple and saw the body as we left for morning prayers. I don't know—"

"Enough. I'll have more questions for you later."

She turned to Father Ailbe, who had just arrived. He was out of breath but walked around the tree, examining the body from every angle.

"Father, is there any reason we need to have this young woman exposed like this?"

"No," he said. "The cause of death is obvious. The heavy rain has washed away any tracks around the trunk. We can bring her down."

Sister Anna took off her own cloak and wrapped it around the corpse as best she could. She then asked Kevin and one of the other brothers to hold the body while she cut the ropes. Once it was released, they lowered it gently and placed it in a patch of grass a few feet away.

"Brother Kevin, can you reach her head?" she asked.

He nodded. He was easily the tallest of the brothers at the monastery. He reached up and began carefully wiggling the head to ease it off the top of the tree. It made a horrible sucking sound when it finally came loose.

"Sister Darerca, may I borrow your veil?"

The abbess was the only one at the monastery who called Dari by her given name.

"Yes, of course."

Dari gave her the linen veil we normally wore around our necks except when we covered our heads at prayer. The abbess folded it in her arms and asked Kevin to place the head there. She began to gently push the hair away from its face, careful to keep it from the bloody stump, so that she could reveal the identity of the young woman. But she already knew. We all knew.

"Saoirse."

The newest member of our monastic family, Saoirse was a strikingly beautiful young woman in her early twenties, from a warrior clan just to the east of the monastery. She had been a student at Kildare and was loved by us all. She was particularly drawn to the stories of the holy women of Egypt who had gone into the desert alone to follow God. Her parents were Christians, and her father was one of the most prosperous cattle lords of our tribe. He was also a proven warrior at the side of the king in battle. He had received generous offers for bridal payments for his daughter since she was twelve, but, being an indulgent man and loving father, he had agreed to the wishes of his child and not made her leave the school. When she turned eighteen, she asked him if she could become a nun. He was none too pleased at first, but he was a devout man with several older sons and daughters. He agreed at last to her marriage to the church and had wept tears of pride as she took her vows at Kildare just a few months earlier. She decided to live as a solitary in a hermitage not far from her family farm. Although she was most sincere in her wish to seek God apart from the world, she came to the church for mass every Sunday and was a frequent visitor to her family's holdings as well.

Sister Anna cradled Saoirse's head in her arms and wrapped the folds of the veil over her face.

"Brother Kevin, can you carry her body back to the infirmary?"

We all walked together back to the monastery, with Sister Anna and Kevin leading the procession. When we reached the infirmary, Kevin carried her body inside. Sister Anna then asked Father Ailbe and me to join her to examine the body.

"Sister Anna, may I send for my grandmother?" I wanted her to look at the signs carved on Saoirse's chest.

"No, Sister Deirdre, you may not."

We entered the hut, and the abbess placed Saoirse's head gently on the side of the examination table next to her body. Father Ailbe began by unwrapping the veil from her face. The look of the young woman was again one of complete peace. I had seen people beheaded before as punishment for some heinous crime. The look that remained on their faces after death was always one of terror.

"No blows to the back of the head or elsewhere on the cranium," said Father Ailbe. "The decapitating blow was made with the single stroke of a broad and very sharp axe. The tendons, vertebrae, and spinal cord were all severed cleanly, with no need for further sawing or cutting. Death was instantaneous. She did not suffer."

He bent down and kissed Saoirse on the forehead, then covered her face with the veil and moved to her body, pulling back the cloak.

"Aside from these symbols carved in her skin, there is no visible trauma to her upper or lower torso. The limbs are similarly unremarkable. Once again, no cuts or lacerations on the hands. The carved symbols show swelling around the edges, indicating that she was alive when they were made."

I helped him turn her over.

"No trauma of any kind to the back of the body."

We turned her over again.

"We should examine her stomach contents," said the abbess.

Father Ailbe and I did the same procedure as with Sister Grainne. The odor was identical.

"Mistletoe."

I covered her again except for her chest. There were six markings artfully carved into her skin. There were two above her breasts, one below, and one to the right and left; these were graceful swirls, figures, and lines of simple design. Between her breasts was a sixth carving twice the size of the others.

"Deirdre, do these symbols mean anything to you?" he asked.

"Yes, Abba, they are druidic signs."

"Signifying what?" asked Sister Anna.

"Sister Anna, I . . . I can't tell you. But I can say that we are all in grave danger. There will be more deaths if we can't find the killer."

She stared at me as if she was weighing something in her mind, then pointed to the sign above Saoirse's right breast.

"This is the head of a crow, the symbol of the Morrigan. Even those of us outside the Order can recognize the sign of the goddess of battle. Do you betray any secrets by confirming this for me?"

"No, you are correct, Sister Anna. It is the symbol of the Morrigan."

"Is there anything else you can tell me about these other signs?"

"Sister Anna, I would if I could, but—"

"Get out, Sister Deirdre."

"But I—"

She held the door open.

"I said leave us. Leave the monastery. Now. You are expelled from the order of holy Brigid. You are no longer one of us."

The whole community of Kildare was gathered outside the infirmary, again waiting for news. They had all heard the final words of Sister Anna. They parted silently as I walked through the crowd. All the brothers and sisters turned their heads away, except for Eithne, who spat at my feet. Only Kevin and Macha reached out to touch my arm as I passed. Dari was at the end of the line and started to hug me, but I shook my head. She was going to have a hard enough time from the others as it was. I walked across the yard to the sleeping quarters of the nuns and took my harp and satchel from the wall above my bed. I left everything else from my life as a nun behind and walked out through the gate, down the path to my grandmother's hut.

Chapter Seven

Would you like some more wine?"

I was sitting by the hearth fire at my grandmother's house that same evening. She had made roasted chicken with apricot sauce, my favorite, and we had just finished washing the dishes.

"No, thank you, Grandmother. I think three cups is enough for one night."

I had a sense of hazy unreality after the events of the day, as if I couldn't wake up from a bad dream—and the wine wasn't helping. I had seen the results of a brutal human sacrifice and been stripped of my life as a nun, all since sunrise. I had come to my grandmother's house because I had nowhere else to go. It had been three years since I had lived in this place. I had gone from here to the monastery after the death of my son because I needed a new life and a new beginning. Kildare had become my home and my world, the nuns and brothers my closest friends. Now all that was gone.

But my personal problems paled in comparison to the deaths of two innocent women and what the future held for us all.

"Grandmother, we need to talk about what to do next."

I had told her about everything that had happened that morning, including a description of the symbols carved onto Saoirse's body. As fellow druids, we could discuss all the details freely without betraying any secrets. If she had been shocked by the murder of Grainne, the sacrifice of Saoirse was even worse. We both knew what it meant and the chain of events that had now been set in motion.

"Yes, we don't have much time. I've sent word to the leading druids throughout Ireland, including Cathbad. The death of Saoirse and the symbols on her body make it clear that Grainne's death was not an isolated incident. The druid who carried out these killings intends to perform the full cycle of sacrifices."

"Is there any way to know the order he intends?" I asked.

"Yes, the sequence was always fixed, assuming that this renegade intends to follow tradition. He's already violated it by using unwilling victims. There were six symbols on her body. He didn't include the death of Grainne since that had been completed. He has already performed the second sacrifice with Saoirse, so that leaves five signs and five more sacrifices. The Triple Death was always the first, followed by the offering to the Morrigan. Tell me again exactly what you saw."

"Six symbols, Grandmother. The first, above her right breast, was the head of a crow."

"Yes, the Morrigan. Saoirse was a sacrifice to the goddess of war. It looks like the murderer hopes to bring about armed conflict."

"The second, over her left breast, was a spiral line circling inward on itself."

"Life. The symbol of the three mother goddesses. That will be the next sacrifice."

"The third was a triangle with a circle in the center."

She shuddered when I said this.

"Blood. The mark of Crom Crúach. We've got to stop this before that sacrifice happens."

"The fourth was two diagonal lines coming together above a small circle."

"Darkness. The sign of Donn, the god of death. It always follows life."

"The fifth symbol was a vertical line with a single horizontal bar across the top, like a Christian cross."

"Light. The emblem of rebirth, holy to the goddess Brigid."

"The last and largest, in the center of her chest, was three lines crossing each other at the center."

"Fire. The sacred sign of the great god Lug. It was always the final sacrifice."

"I told Sister Anna that more deaths were coming so that she could take precautions. I hope I didn't reveal too much."

"No, my child, it was the right thing to do. We can't betray the secrets of the druids, but we have to protect the lives of our friends at Kildare."

"Grandmother, who would do such a thing?"

"That's the question King Dúnlaing is going to ask me tomorrow. He sent a messenger just before you arrived, saying he wants to see me at his farm in the morning."

"I'll come with you, if you'd like."

"Don't be too eager. It isn't going to be a cordial meeting. Dúnlaing is furious at the druids for letting this happen. Since, for better or worse, I'm the best-known druid in the province of Leinster, I'm afraid his anger is going to be focused on me."

"Maybe I can mollify him. I think he's always liked me."

"Yes, but liking you isn't going to make up for two dead subjects at the hands of some deranged druid. He knows these murders threaten his power as king. He's going to be looking for people to blame. You might become a target of his rage as well."

"I can bear that. But what do we tell him?"

"We can say that the killer is a druid," she said. "We can say that there are more sacrifices coming if we don't stop him. None of this betrays any druid secrets."

"But which druid could be carrying out these murders?"

"What do you think, Deirdre? I have my ideas, but you've always been a clever girl."

I thought for a moment.

"My first guess would be someone from one of the fundamentalist factions. They don't have many followers, but those they do have are committed. Ever since Patrick arrived, there have been a few druids who have seen Christianity as a threat to their way of life. There have never been any deaths or even violence, but there has been resentment building for a long time. Honestly, though, I don't know why they would be worried. In the decades since the Gospel arrived on this island, Christianity has barely managed to survive. The monks at Armagh like to say Patrick converted thousands to the faith, but I doubt he baptized more than a few hundred during all the years of his mission. A few whole clans, like Saoirse's family, have become Christians, but mostly it's been a single person here and there."

"And of those who do convert," Grandmother added, "the most sincere often become celibate monks and nuns. Not exactly a recipe for growth. You need children for a religion to be successful."

"That's true. And there aren't even that many monks and nuns in Ireland. Kildare has no more than a few dozen.

Armagh has more than us, but not many. There are maybe a half dozen other monasteries scattered around the island, but there can't be more than a few hundred of us—of them—in total. Maybe there are two thousand Christians in Ireland all together, but we're not exactly growing by leaps and bounds. I don't know how long we can survive as a faith before people give up and return to the old ways. And now, as if we weren't failing on our own, someone is killing nuns. I don't think that is going to help our recruitment efforts."

"That may be the point," she said. "The killer may be hoping to bring Christianity to an end in one grand and horrible bloodbath."

"If it is one of the fanatical druids," I said, "Finian would know—if it isn't Finian himself."

She took a sip from her own wine cup.

"That was my first thought as well. That young man is a gifted sacrificer and deeply committed to the old ways. He's also a lightning rod for the miscreant and malcontent druids on the island. Most of them don't have the brains to organize these killings, but Finian would."

"What if it isn't Finian or his followers?" I asked. "What if someone else is pulling the strings? Maybe these murders are a political attack aimed at the king but disguised as a religious crusade. It would be a clever way to bring Dúnlaing down, by attacking his credibility to control events in his own kingdom."

"That would be devious. Dúnlaing has many enemies, as does any powerful king. Are you thinking about the Uí Néill?"

"Yes. They've pushed our border back to the Liffey in the north. Their forces are as exhausted as ours, but if they could destroy Dúnlaing without a fight they would welcome the chance to expand their control into Leinster."

"And then there's the abbot of Armagh."

"Yes," I sighed. "He's part of the Uí Néill royal family. If he could extend the political power of his people, he could also increase his own dominance. He would like nothing more than to see the monastery of Kildare in ruins. When I saw him a few months ago, he told me he'd like to kill us all."

"Was that before or after you held a knife to his throat?" she chuckled.

"Before, I think. Anyway, I made a powerful enemy for us that day."

"But," she said, "the Uí Néill are not the only political threat to Dúnlaing. There are plenty of kings in Leinster and Munster who would like to see him fall, including the young ruler of Glendalough."

"No. Cormac would never harm the nuns of Kildare. He's as ambitious a man who ever lived, but that is a line he wouldn't cross."

"I agree, but other royalty might not have such high standards, including Dúnlaing's own sons."

"True, though in any case none of the kings, princes, or abbots of Ireland would have the knowledge necessary to perform these sacrifices on their own. They would have to have found a druid who was willing to desecrate and defile everything we stand for. I can't imagine any druid would do that for the sake of money or power—or for any other reason."

"I can't imagine it either," she said, "but you never know what lies in the heart of another person."

We stared at the fire for a long time without speaking. It had grown dark outside and there was no moon to brighten the night.

"Grandmother, I am going to find whoever did this. I may not be a member of the monastery anymore, but Sister Anna gave me a job to do and I intend to carry it through. The nuns of Kildare are still my sisters in my heart. This killer may not stop with the solitaries scattered around the woods. Macha could be a target next, or Garwain—or even Dari. I swear by holy Brigid and the gods of my tribe that I will destroy this man. Maybe not being a nun could even help me in the search. I'm not constrained by the rules of the monastery or the authority of Sister Anna. I'm free now to wander anywhere on this island with my standing as a druid and a bard. I can make kings answer to me if I need to."

"True, my child. But you still look like a nun."

I got up from the hearth and went to the large wooden chest at the foot of my old bed. I untied the belt around my waist and laid it on the bed, then reached over my shoulders and pulled off my rough woolen tunic. As I stood there naked, I folded my garments from the church at Kildare and put them into the chest. Then I reached to the bottom and took out one of the fine linen tunics I had stored away three years earlier and put it on, along with a broad belt of worked leather. Then I took the solid gold torque I had been given by King Dúnlaing himself as a badge of office and fixed it around my neck. Finally, I reached into the chest and pulled out the beautifully woven multicolored robe of a bard and threw it over my shoulders, then fastened it with a stylized horsehead brooch made of Spanish silver and studded with lapis lazuli.

My grandmother came over and put her arms around me. Only my small wooden cross remained as a symbol of my life as a nun.

"It doesn't really match the rest of your outfit," she said.

I reached behind my neck and started to untie the lanyard, but then stopped. Instead, I tucked the cross inside my tunic close to my heart.

"It's still a part of me. I'm going to keep it on, at least for now."

Grandmother kissed my cheek.

"Well, we should get some sleep," she said. "We've got to face a very angry king tomorrow."

Chapter Eight

The feasting hall of King Dúnlaing on the banks of the Liffey a few miles from the monastery was the largest in all of Leinster. Like most buildings in Ireland, it was a round wattle-and-daub hut with a peaked thatched roof, but its scale was grander than any other structure I had ever seen, save for the oaken church of holy Brigid at Kildare. The two guards at the door bowed as my grandmother and I entered the single room lighted by a roaring fire in the central hearth and a hole in the peak of the roof that also allowed smoke to escape. The walls were covered with shields, swords, and the preserved heads of slain enemies. There were enough sturdy wooden tables and benches to seat at least two hundred men, but it was empty that morning except for the king, who was seated in his chair at the head table, eating breakfast.

He rose to greet us. I had known him my whole life and had sung for him and his warriors many times at feasts in this same hall. He was a tall, straight-backed man about seventy years old with green eyes and white hair down to his shoulders. It was plain to anyone that he was no longer the young warrior who had held this kingdom together for almost fifty years. The lines in his face were now deep and his right hand would tremble when he became tired, but his mind was as sharp as ever and his spirit unfaltering.

"Aoife, Deirdre, welcome. Would you like some breakfast?"

He was always a gracious host, but I knew his invitation was a formality today. I could see the strain and worry in his eyes. I couldn't imagine what it was like to be a king and have the burdens of a whole people resting on my shoulders. Once after a feast when he had drained many cups of mead and we were sitting together alone by the fire in this very hall, he had spoken more freely to me than he ever had before, perhaps more than he had ever spoken with anyone. He said that to be a king is to be a servant, with less freedom than the lowliest slave. It was, he quickly added, a great honor to care for his people, a privilege granted to him by the gods, but there were times he would have traded it all to be a simple farmer tending a small plot of land in a quiet valley and watching the sun set in peace each evening.

"No, thank you, my lord," said my grandmother. "We ate some bread and cheese along the way."

"Sit, then," he said. "We have much to discuss."

We sat together on the bench to his right, the place of honor.

"Two nuns are dead, murdered by a druid," he began. "I have received reports on both from Sister Anna, but I want to know every detail from the two of you. You were both there when the first body was brought to the monastery. Deirdre, you were there for the second. Tell me everything now."

We told him.

When we had finished, he closed his eyes. He had taken in every word, interrupting us several times to ask questions about both women. Then he opened his eyes and leaned forward toward us.

"Aoife, I know there is no such thing as a chief druid. The members of the Order operate independently, governed only by tradition and common consent. But I also know you are the most respected druid in my kingdom and indeed all of Leinster. You probably know more about what is going on in this land than I do. I do not ask you to betray the secrets of the druids, but I want you to tell me if you have heard anything about who might be responsible for this outrage."

"No, my lord, I regret that I have not. As you say, there is no individual or council that governs the druids, but we are in constant communication with each other, arranging religious events, coordinating activities, seeking advice. There is scarcely a chicken sacrificed anywhere in this province that I and all my fellow druids don't know about beforehand. But regarding these horrible events there was no word, no whisper that such a thing was coming."

He turned to look at me.

"Deirdre, I heard that Sister Anna expelled you from the monastery and I'm sorry. I make it a point not to interfere in the affairs of Christians, but perhaps I can speak to her at some point in the future. For now, I have greater problems to deal with. A killer is stalking the nuns of Kildare. I have already sent word to the abbess ordering her to bring all the solitary sisters into the walls of the monastery. I was not surprised to discover that she had issued the same command herself hours earlier. I have sent a dozen of my best warriors to guard the monastery walls at all times. No one aside from the sisters and brothers and those well known to them will be allowed inside until this is over."

"A wise precaution," I said. "Thank you, my lord. I will sleep better knowing that my friends are safe."

"Frankly, Deirdre, I would be pleased if you didn't sleep at all. I know the abbess placed you in charge of finding the killer before she removed you from Kildare. Her commission may have expired when you stopped being a nun, but if I know you, it won't matter. In any case, I'm giving you the same mandate by my own authority—find the man who murdered these nuns and stop him before he kills anyone else. You are a druid, and now that you're wearing those bardic robes again, you will command even greater respect among the people of this kingdom. You have my permission to use any resources and any means necessary to accomplish this. But if you find out who is responsible, you are to tell me immediately and let me deal with him. By my authority as king, I tell you both that there will be no secret druid trial for this man. He will be dealt with by me in a very public manner. Do you understand?"

"Yes, my lord," I said.

"Good. I hope I don't need to explain to either of you the consequences for this kingdom if the killer is not found soon. You may have thought about how this turmoil makes us vulnerable to outside forces, but it may also tear apart our people from within. Saoirse's father is a Christian and one of my finest warriors, in spite of your strange command to love your enemies. His clan is just one of a dozen in this kingdom, but he commands great respect, and others will follow his lead. He was here last night, threatening to personally burn down every druid grove and temple in the land if his daughter's murderer is not found. I understand his anger. If it were my beloved child who had suffered such a fate, I would stop at nothing, not even a king's command, to get revenge. But the western clans in my kingdom have sired many druids and are fervent patrons of the old ways. If they or their holy places are attacked, there will be clan war. It is my duty as king to hold my people together. If we begin to fight among ourselves, we might as well hand the kingdom over to the Uí Néill. I respect the religious traditions of my people, whether they follow the old ways or your Jesus, but I cannot allow our tribe to fall into civil war. Before I permit this kingdom to be divided, I will expel all the druids from my kingdom."

"My lord," said my grandmother, "you can't be serious."

"I have never been more serious in my life. I have no desire to abandon the ways of my fathers, but I will not side with the Order if it sacrifices innocent girls or is unable to stop one of its members from performing such deeds. Do I make myself clear?"

"Yes, my lord."

The king rose from his chair and bade us farewell, then left the feasting hall. My grandmother and I remained seated, too dismayed to stand up.

"Do you think he would really expel the druids, Grandmother?"

"Yes, my child. If it comes to choosing sides in a clan war, I'm afraid that's exactly what he would do. He can't allow the Christians of his kingdom to be slaughtered while he stands idly by. But this is not good news for anyone, even followers of your faith. A religious war in the kingdom of Dúnlaing would bring chaos on our land. The hungry wolves from the other kingdoms would then come and pick clean our bones."

"What can we do?" I asked.

"Find the murderer, Deirdre. And find him quickly."

Chapter Nine

My grandmother and I were back at her home by early afternoon. On the walk back from King Dúnlaing's feasting hall, we discussed what I should do first and decided the best course of action was to immediately confront Finian, the leader of the conservative druids. He lived on a small holding near the ancient fort of Dún Ailinne, so I decided I could leave early the next morning and be back home by nightfall. I wasn't worried about meeting him or wandering the pathways of Leinster alone. I was a bard, a sacred person in the eyes of all. To kill a bard was to destroy the history and memories of a people, and so was unthinkable on our island. Finian and his fanatical band might despise me for being a Christian, but they would never harm me.

Just after we returned and I had poured a cool glass of buttermilk for both of us, I heard a knock on the door. I opened it and much to my delight found Dari, with Kevin there beside her. We hugged each other and I invited them both in.

"I'm going to wait outside, if you don't mind, Deirdre," said Kevin. "I'm responsible for guarding Dari and I want to keep an eye open out here in case anyone comes near."

"My hero," said Dari, and she stood on her toes to give Kevin a kiss on his cheek. He blushed like a schoolgirl.

We both laughed. We needed to laugh with all that had happened the last few days. I poured Dari a cup of buttermilk, and my grandmother took one to Kevin as well. She went out to milk her cow and weed the cabbages in the garden, leaving Dari and me alone in her hut.

"How are things going at the monastery?" I asked.

"Not well, as you might expect. The place is in a panic after the two murders, and everyone is wondering what will happen next. It feels like a fortress with the king's men posted at the gates and walls, though at least we don't have to worry about being killed in our beds."

"How is Father Ailbe?"

"He's wonderful, like a calm harbor in a storm. He's worried, of course, but he has a comforting word for everyone. It's Sister Anna I'm concerned about."

"Sister Anna? I would have thought she would be stronger than anyone."

"She is, at least as far as she lets anyone see. But I know she's feeling the loss of Grainne and Saoirse terribly and worries about the other sisters."

"I'm surprised she allowed you to visit me after what happened yesterday."

"Actually, she doesn't know I'm here. But the nuns are permitted to leave the monastery grounds during the day with one of the brothers if he's armed."

"What will she do if she finds out you came to see me?"

"I don't know, and I'm certainly not going to tell her. She doesn't have the authority to excommunicate you, Deirdre, just remove you as a nun. On the other hand, I wouldn't show up at the church anytime soon if I were you, especially dressed like that. You look magnificent, by the way. I've never seen you dressed in anything but our dull nun clothes. You make quite an impression."

"I hope so. It might serve me well in my current task."

I told her about my visit to the king and his commission to find the killer.

"I'll help you, Deirdre. We'll work together."

"Thanks, Dari, but Sister Anna won't let you run around the countryside with me."

"I don't care. She can kick me out of the order too, if she wants. In fact, I might leave in any case. I can't stand the thought of being at Kildare without you."

"Dari," I said, "don't be foolish. Kildare is your home. I'm not going to be responsible for your leaving all that behind."

"I don't want to leave the monastery, but it's not the same without you there."

"Are the others being unkind to you for being my friend?"

"Some are a bit cold, but not exactly unkind—well, except for Eithne, who has managed to say 'I told you so about Deirdre' at least ten times since yesterday. I'm ready to pound her with a frying pan."

"Forget Eithne. How are the solitaries doing inside the monastery?"

"That's one of the things weighing on Sister Anna. Even with all that's happened, most of them refuse to come to Kildare. They say they'll trust in God to protect them."

"They're ignoring the orders of the king?"

"I think they're more afraid of Sister Anna than the king, but they won't even come to the monastery for her sake. The problem is that they're uncomfortable living with other people. Many of them have been alone for years. It's a terrifying thought for them to suddenly move into crowded sleeping quarters with other nuns. In fact, those few solitaries who have come to the monastery have settled into other buildings so they can be by themselves. I think Sister Coleen has set up her bed in the nook above the granary."

"What about Riona?"

Sister Riona was a solitary who lived about a mile from my grandmother's home. She was a cousin of mine on my mother's side, a couple of years younger than me, and a much better nun than I had ever been. Her grandfather had been a druid, though she never knew him. Her father and mother had become Christians before she was born and encouraged Riona in her desire to be a sister of holy Brigid. She was an only child, so when they died a few years ago she moved back into the family home as a solitary. She raised sheep there and gave the meat and wool to the monastery.

"She's one of those who has refused to come to Kildare," Dari said. "Sister Anna told me to visit her and try to persuade her to return. It's nearby, so I'm on my way there now."

"Let me come with you. Maybe she'll listen to a kinswoman. I don't like the thought of her out there alone. If she doesn't want to go to the monastery, I'll see if she wants to stay here with my grandmother and me."

"I'd be grateful. She's as sweet as can be, but there's a stubborn streak in your family."

"Not stubborn, Dari, just . . . determined."

We laughed again and went out the door. Kevin was taking his role as protector very seriously, marching back and forth in front of the hut as if the Saxons were about to invade.

"Kevin, I'm going with Dari to Riona's hermitage to see if I can't talk her into returning to Kildare. You can wait here until I bring her back. Maybe you could help my grandmother in the garden. Dari will be safe with me."

He scratched his head.

"Well, I don't know, Deirdre. Sister Anna told me to guard her. Are you sure you'll be safe? I mean, I don't want anything to happen to *either* of you."

Kevin was one of the best men I knew. He was loyal and brave and kind, not to mention tall and handsome. If he hadn't been such a pious monk, I would have invited him into my bed years ago.

"Please don't worry, Kevin," I said. "You know that no one would dare to touch a bard or anyone under their protection. If it makes you feel better, I'll take a sword with me."

"All right, but please promise you'll be back here before dark."

"I promise."

I told my grandmother where we were going and took my father's sword from the wall near my bed. I knew no one would bother us, but I wasn't going to take any chances.

The path to Riona's farm lay through a forest of sweet-smelling aspen trees to the west. The heavy rain from the day before had stopped and the sky was warm and clear as we drew near to Riona's farm. Her small flock was in the meadow next to her house.

"You'd better let me go first, Dari. Her dogs know me."

At that moment five large sheepdogs came rushing down the hill, barking at us. They stopped a few feet in front of us, snarling and teeth showing, with the hair on the back of their necks raised.

"It's all right, boys. It's me, Deirdre."

I held out my hand for them to smell. The largest one almost took it off.

"I thought you said they knew you."

"Maybe they don't recognize me in my robes."

"Rory, stop! It's all right, lads. They're friends."

Riona was coming from the barn behind us, pushing a large handcart in front of her. The dogs all ran up to her, and she scratched them behind the ears, then came over to give us both a big hug.

"Look at you, Deirdre, dressed up like the chief bard of Ireland. I'm so glad to see you two. How's Aunt Aoife?"

"Fine. I left her with Kevin pulling weeds."

"Well, come in and have a cup of mead. I have to bring the sheep in soon, but I have a little while. I had two lambs taken by wolves last week, so I've been keeping them all in the pen by the house at night."

We went into her home, which was almost identical to my grandmother's. Riona once said she had thought about knocking it down and building a proper little hermit's hut, but it seemed silly to waste a good building that had been in her family for years.

She poured us a cup and we sat down around her table.

"So, are you here to give me the same message the king's men did yesterday?"

"Yes," I said. "You know about the killings and that the murderer is planning more. This is serious business, Riona. You're all alone out here. Please come back to the monastery where you'll be safe, just until this is all over. If you don't want to do that, then come and stay with me and my grandmother at her house."

She took a long drink of the mead.

"Deirdre, I appreciate your concern, I really do, but I'm not leaving. I can't take care of my sheep if I'm hiding in the monastery or even at Aunt Aoife's house. The wolves will have them all for breakfast before the week is out."

"I'm sure we could find a local farmer to keep them for a little while," Dari said.

"Maybe, but they're my sheep. I was there when each of them was born. I take care of them, watch them, shear them, and I'm the one who gently eases them from this life when the time comes. They know me. I can't just drop them off at some stranger's farm."

"Could you bring them to Grandmother's house and watch them there?"

"That wouldn't work. She isn't set up for sheep. You don't have the pens or anything else they need. Besides, they're happy here."

"Riona," I said, "there is a vicious, determined murderer roaming these woods who is hunting nuns and sacrificing them in horrible ways. I understand your love for your animals, but are they worth your life?"

"I think you overestimate this druid killer, Deirdre. He got away with killing two women who lived without any protection, but I've got five dogs who would rip out someone's throat at my command. I also know how to use a sword. My father was a warrior, just like yours."

She refilled our cups and took another drink.

"And besides," she continued, "I can't give in to fear of the druids. I've lived with it my whole life."

"What do you mean?" asked Dari.

"My grandfather was a druid sacrificer," she said. "He left this home before I was born, but I heard the story from my parents. When they had been married just a short time, they decided to become Christians. They had attended the monastery school together and loved the life of the church, but would never have dreamed in their youth of defying their parents and leaving the old ways behind. But by the time they came of age and married, only my grandfather was still alive. He lived here with them and served the Order at ceremonies all over the province. He was a formidable man, they say, tall and powerful. It must have taken a great deal of courage for my father and mother to tell him that day that they were joining the church."

"What did he do?" I asked. I had heard bits and pieces of this story from my grandmother over the years, but never the whole tale.

"He stood up from this table and raised his arms to the sky. Then he called on the gods to curse them, to wither their crops, to decimate their flocks, to render my mother barren, to make them suffer every possible torment for the rest of their lives, then to die wrapped in flame, along with anyone they loved."

"Dear Jesus, that's horrible!" Dari said. "What happened then?"

"He walked out the door and never returned. I was born four years later, but not before my mother suffered three miscarriages, and the two of them almost starved after their harvest failed twice and the flock was wiped out by a blight. They thought everything was fine after that and the curse had run its course, but when I came home from the monastery to visit them one day, I found their bodies in the charred ruins of the old barn. I don't know how the fire had started or why they couldn't get out, but I buried them in the meadow and moved here myself to tend the sheep."

"I heard that your grandfather left Ireland years ago," I said.

"Yes, I heard that too. They say he went to Argyll in the land of the Picts with the Dál Riata. I heard later that he had gone to the northern isles. He may still be alive somewhere. I don't know and I don't care. He was a wicked man who killed my parents."

Tears were rolling down her cheeks.

"I can't let him win. I can't let this farm go to ruin because of a curse or a mad druid on the loose. Deirdre, you know I love you and Aunt Aoife. I have nothing against the druids. Every one of them I've ever met was kind and generous to me. But there are some bad apples in your basket, like my grandfather, who use whatever powers the forces of this earth have given them to cause pain and death."

Dari and I both put our hands on hers.

"Riona," Dari said, "I understand. I'll tell Sister Anna why you won't come to the monastery. She won't like it, but I'll tell her you're well protected here. Is there anything we can bring to you?"

She wiped her eyes.

"No, thank you. I'll be fine. This has just been a hard time with the deaths of Grainne and Saoirse."

Dari and I bade her farewell and walked down the path to my grandmother's house in silence for a while before Dari spoke.

"Do you think she'll be safe?" Dari asked.

"Yes, I hope so. No one is going to get near that house with those dogs."

I looked behind me to the southwest.

"The sun is getting low in the sky. You and Kevin had better get back to the monastery before Sister Anna sends out the king's guards to look for you."

"True enough. Will you be all right? I hate to leave you."

"I'll be fine."

"Be careful tomorrow with Finian. He may be a fanatic, but he's as cunning as they come."

"Don't worry, Dari, I'll be fine. He would never hurt a fellow druid."

Chapter Ten

Finian lived alone on the edge of King Dúnlaing's territory in a hut tucked away beneath an oak grove in the shadow of an ancient dolmen. Some Christians called these piles of giant rocks druid altars, but they were never used for sacrifices. The stories passed down from long ago said they were the tombs of famous kings.

I had known Finian for many years, but I would never have called him a friend. He was a few years older than me and had been one of the best students at the monastery school. His parents were not Christians, but neither were they particularly devoted to the old ways. Many non-Christians sent their children to Kildare, and we never tried to proselytize them. Part of our mission of service was teaching, and we were happy to provide a free education to anyone. Reading, writing, mathematics, science, literature—these were our subjects, not religion. Father Ailbe taught special classes in the Christian faith after school for students who wanted to attend, but these were optional. Finian, however, was always there, listening, asking questions, and debating the finer points of theology with Father Ailbe. Most of us assumed he would be baptized when he finished school and perhaps even become a priest, but one day when he was seventeen he disappeared. It wasn't until months later that we heard he had joined the Order and was training at a druidic school on Rathlin Island off the northern coast of Ulster. When he returned home to Leinster five years later, he was a sacrificer and a committed member of a small traditionalist group who sought to purify the teachings of the druids of all outside influences. I had seen him occasionally over the years at ceremonies. Kings would often call on him to perform the most important sacrifices, since he was more skilled than anyone else at the dispatching of animal victims and the interpretation of their entrails. Whenever I had tried to speak to him at these events, he always turned away.

He was in front of his house at a small stone altar, holding a dove in his hands. His head was shaved in front from ear to ear, in the manner of male members of the Order. He wore the scarlet robes of a druid sacrificer over his white tunic and a gold torque around his neck. What set him apart from every other druid priest I had ever met were his tattoos. On his cheeks and arms were intricate spirals and colored animal figures in a manner not seen in many years.

"Greetings, Finian. May the gods grant you peace this fine day," I said in the formal manner of address to a fellow druid.

He turned to look at me with his piercing blue eyes and scowled.

"That would mean something, Deirdre, if you actually believed in the gods."

"May I speak with you, Finian?"

"Be silent until I finish this sacrifice."

He took the dove and raised it in both hands to the sky, uttering prayers in a form of Irish so old, I scarcely understood the words. Then in one swift motion he took his knife and cut off the head of the bird, letting the blood fall onto the stones below. He then sliced open the creature and removed its liver and other internal organs. He probed them with his fingers for several minutes while I waited patiently. At last he placed the entire carcass of the bird into the fire next to the altar as a holocaust offering.

"Are the portents good?" I asked.

He wiped his hands and knife on a cloth and said a final prayer before turning to me, knife tucked firmly into his belt.

"The signs are unclear today."

"Do you perform this sacrifice every day?"

"Many in the Order, even sacrificers, no longer perform the morning offering. I find that omission appalling. Why are you here?"

"Have you heard of the deaths of the two nuns of Kildare?"

"Of course. Do you think news like that hasn't spread to the far corners of Ireland by now?"

"Undoubtedly. Who do you think might be responsible?"

"Well, shall we consider this rationally, like we used to in Sister Anna's logic class?"

"Fine."

"We know that only druids have the knowledge to perform sacrifices. The women in question were killed by means of sacrifice. Therefore the women were killed by a druid."

"So you agree that there are no other possible suspects, aside from druids?"

"The only other possibility is that a druid taught someone else to perform the sacrifices. I think that unlikely in the extreme. No druid in his right mind, even in the Order's present state of corruption, would reveal such secrets to those who are not initiated. Such a thing has never happened in all the centuries of our race."

"Which druid do you think is responsible?"

"Instead of playing this little game, Deirdre, why don't you just ask me what you came to ask?"

"All right, Finian. Did you kill those two nuns?"

"No."

"Do you know who did?"

"No."

"Why should I believe you?"

"You shouldn't. It's reasonable to assume that whichever druid killed the nuns chose his targets because he resents Christianity. Now, since most druids on this island are all too eager to welcome Christians, I would say the killer takes a narrower, more traditional view. It's well known that I am a traditionalist—or what you undoubtedly refer to as a fanatic—and that I have no love for your church. So if I were you, I'd put me on the top of your list of suspects."

"But you didn't do it?"

"I already told you that. Is there anything else you want?"

"Yes. You should know that King Dúnlaing has put me in charge of finding the killer. I need to warn you that he will not tolerate a lack of cooperation in my investigation. If you have any knowledge of these crimes or hear anything without reporting it to me, he is likely to consider you as guilty as the killer, even if you never touched those nuns."

"Do you plan to bring me before the king for interrogation?"

"No. But my warning holds. If you know anything, you should tell me now."

"Even if I did know something, I wouldn't betray those who believe as I do. I didn't kill the nuns, but I sympathize with the man who did. I understand the anger that would drive a person of faith to kill and risk his own death for his beliefs. If I thought sacrificing a few nuns would remove the stench of Christianity from this land, I would do it in a heartbeat and gladly face whatever punishment was meted out to me by the king."

"Finian, what happened to you? You were one of the best students at the monastery school. You experienced nothing but love from the sisters and brothers of Kildare. Why have you turned on us? What did we do to you?"

I had never seen the expression on anyone's face that I saw then on Finian's. If it is possible to combine unbounded hatred and infinite delight into one malevolent, triumphant look, that was what I saw.

"You think that I rejected Christianity because of something that happened to me at the school? You think perhaps I resent the way Sister Anna rapped my knuckles with a switch when I passed notes in class? Or maybe that one of the brothers forced me behind the barn and made me perform unnatural acts with him? Not at all. Everyone treated me with great respect and kindness, just as the Gospels taught them to."

"Then why?"

"Because I realized at last that Christianity is poison. Its message seems so innocent at first—Love your neighbor as yourself, forgive your enemies, look forward to heaven someday. But I want to live in the real world. The truth is that life is a struggle, full of suffering. Whatever joy we experience in life, we make for ourselves and those we love. We can't waste our lives on our knees hoping for better times. We are born in blood and die in pain. To ignore that and believe that a single, all-powerful, and benevolent God controls our fate is both ignorant and foolish. Do you think the wisdom gained over untold ages and passed down through our traditions is to be cast aside because a Jewish rabbi said some pleasing words on a mountain? Your Jesus claimed that a little yeast leavens a whole lump of dough. Well, Christianity is that yeast and it spreads its oh-so-innocent teachings into our most cherished traditions. Your religion will never amount to anything on this island, but it corrupts everything that it touches."

I stood there not knowing what to say.

"And you, Deirdre, you're the most dangerous one of all, nun or not. Look at you in your robes, a bard of the greatest skill and the noblest rank. Yet you have turned your back on the ways of your people in a futile attempt to be both a Christian and a druid. I can at least respect someone like Sister Anna who tells me to my face that I'm going to hell for serving false gods. But you want to have it both ways. You'd have us all, Christians and druids, join hands around the altar of the gods with a little cross on top enjoying the best of both worlds. Well, you're a fool, and I despise you and everything you stand for."

With that, he turned his back on me and walked away.

Chapter Eleven

I didn't trust Finian. If he wasn't the killer, it was surely someone from his small group of fellow believers; and if so, I couldn't believe that Finian didn't know who it was. I decided that I would go back to my grandmother's house for a satchel of food and a blanket, then return the next day to the grove where Finian lived and keep an eye on him. If he left his farm, I would follow him, sword in hand, and stop the next killing before it happened. There was a small hill covered with leafy trees behind the dolmen that would be perfect for keeping an eye on him. I had spent many hours in my youth stalking deer with my bow and arrow, so I knew how to stay out of sight.

Just as I was leaving the next morning, Dari and Kevin walked down the path.

"I wanted to see how your visit with Finian went."

"About as you would expect. He denied everything, but I'm going back to his grove to keep an eye on him for a few days."

"Would you make a detour with us first?"

"To where?"

"Pelagia's hut. One of the king's men went there yesterday morning to bring her back to the monastery, but she wouldn't even talk to him. You know her better than I do, and you can speak to her in Greek."

"Nobody really knows her, Dari."

Pelagia was a small, elderly solitary who lived on a crannog in a lake southeast of the monastery. Crannogs were artificial islands built for defense centuries ago in lakes and rivers. In times of trouble, people would retreat to them, but the one Pelagia lived on was too small to be of practical use and so had been deserted for ages when she built her hermitage there. It was connected to the shore only by a rickety wooden bridge that threatened to collapse at any moment.

Pelagia herself seemed ageless to me the few times I had visited her. She was a true solitary and never came to the monastery. She spent her time tending her garden and praying. The rumor was that long ago she had been a wealthy prostitute in the Syrian city of Antioch but one day had heard the preaching of a local bishop and abandoned her profession to become a nun—or rather a monk. Pelagia always dressed as a man and even cut her hair short. Indeed, until she spoke, which she seldom did, you wouldn't guess that she was a woman at all. She had lived on her little island since before Father Ailbe had arrived at Kildare. He would visit her once a year to offer her the Eucharist and hear her confession. They always spoke in Greek, since she had never learned more than a few words of Irish. I always wondered how she had ended up in Ireland, but even Father Ailbe didn't know and I respected her privacy too much to ask. Though no one knew her well, she was revered as a holy woman among Christians and non-Christians alike.

"Please, Deirdre, it's not far out of your way. Sister Anna is getting more worried about the solitaries who refuse to come to the monastery. If I can't convince Pelagia, I'm afraid the abbess is going to send the king's warriors to force her to return."

"All right, I'll go with you. Kevin, I presume you're coming along to escort them back?"

"Yes. I've been practicing with my sword, so I'm ready for anything."

He then proceeded to demonstrate his skill by attacking a large holly bush. He looked so much like a little boy playing soldier that we couldn't help but laugh. He wasn't a particularly talented swordsman, but he was big and very strong. I wouldn't have wanted to face him on a battlefield.

It started raining buckets just as we came to the far side of Pelagia's lake. I had somehow taken the wrong path so that we ended up pushing our way through reeds in water up to our waists. I had never been so thoroughly wet. Even Dari was looking forlorn. We were ready to give up on finding the path when we saw two men in a log boat paddling along the shallows. I called to them and they pulled close to shore. They invited us to stay and eat with them in their hut just a short distance away until the rain stopped. We gladly accepted.

Their home was little more than a shed covered with a thatched roof. Still, I was grateful to sit in front of their blazing fire. Kevin positioned himself near the door as our faithful guard. Dari curled up in a dry corner to take a nap until dinner was ready.

The fishermen were a strange-looking pair, one tall and lanky while the other was short and rather stout. I had known many peasants and woodsmen in my day, but these two were something from another age. Instead of woolen cloaks and pants, they wore only a kind of long tunic made from animal skins. They had no furniture of even the simplest kind, but sat and slept on deerskins covered with fleece. The only metal I saw in their hut was a small bronze cauldron and an ancient iron blade they used to fillet fish, which seemed to be their only food aside from wild herbs and a gray paste made of acorns. Still, the stew they were making smelled delicious, so I wasn't about to complain.

I tried to engage them in conversation, but their Irish was strange, as if from long ago and seldom spoken. They communicated with each other mostly through gestures, but they were friendly and made me feel welcome. As the stew began to bubble, the taller one looked at me and spoke.

"Ma'am, if I could ask, what's that hanging from your neck? I've never seen one before."

My cross had fallen out of my tunic while we were stumbling through the marsh.

"It's my cross. I was a sister of the monastery of holy Brigid at Kildare."

They looked puzzled. I was amazed they hadn't heard of Brigid's monastery. It was only a few miles from their lake, though they had probably never been far from home.

"It's a community of women and men," I continued, "who have devoted their lives to the worship of God and service of others."

"Which god would that be, ma'am?"

"You don't need to keep calling me 'ma'am'—but to answer your question, we worship the Christian God, creator of heaven and earth, who sent his son Jesus to show us the way of salvation."

The shorter one reached over to stir the pot, which was now boiling. He threw in a handful of herbs, glanced over at his companion, then looked back at me.

"Sometimes we pray to the gods when the fishing isn't good, but we never heard of yours. Does he live under the earth?"

I was astonished. I knew that most of the people in Ireland still followed the old ways, but I thought everyone had at least heard of Jesus. How had we Christians failed so badly?

"You've never heard of the Christian God? But you live on the same lake as Pelagia, one of our nuns."

"Oh, the holy lady," the taller one said. "She never talks to us. We don't really go anywhere else. We mostly stay by the lake."

I decided I was going to teach these men the basics of Christianity before dinner.

"Well, our God made the earth and sky—even this lake you live on. He made the animals and birds and fish. He sends rain and sunshine and loves us all. A long time ago, he became a man named Jesus and died for our sins so that we could go to heaven if we put our trust in him."

They were silent for a long time. Then the shorter one cleared his throat.

"You mean your god is dead?"

"No, no." I clarified. "He was dead for three days, but then he came back to life and went to heaven to live with his father, the one true God Christians believe in."

"But isn't his son a true god too?"

"Yes, of course, but you see, God is divided into three parts— the Father, the Son, and the Holy Spirit."

The taller one scratched his head.

"I thought you just said there was only one god. Now you're saying there's three?"

I sighed deeply and wondered how I could explain the Trinity to these two. I decided to use an old trick of Patrick's.

"Look at this clover," I said as I reached to a bed of shamrocks just outside the door. I plucked one out and held it up to them. "It has three distinct leaves, but it is still a single plant. In the same way, God is three persons, but also a unity."

I could see their puzzled faces as they pondered this. At last the shorter one spoke up.

"But don't some clovers have four leaves? My grandpa always said those were lucky."

"It's not about the clover!" I was out of patience now, as well as being hungry. "It's an analogy, a metaphor," I practically yelled at them. "It's a way of explaining a cosmic mystery so that even people like you can understand it!"

They looked at each other uncomfortably. I leaned forward and put my head in my hands, ashamed at being such a poor guest.

"Well, ma'am, like I said, we don't get away from the lake too much."

After dinner, our hosts led us to the path that went around the lake to Pelagia's hermitage. There was smoke coming from behind her hut.

"*Chaire, Pelagia*," I called out my greeting in Greek.

There was only silence.

I pulled out my sword and motioned for Kevin and Dari to stay behind me. Kevin instead stepped in front of me onto the bridge with his weapon held ready. I was perturbed but followed him. I was also afraid the bridge might collapse under his weight.

He entered her hut first, with me and then Dari close behind. We could tell at a glance that it was empty. There was no bed, only a mat on the dirt floor covered by an old woolen blanket. A cross made from reeds hung on the wall next to—oddly enough—a strand of gorgeous pearls. There was nothing else in the small hermitage except for an old cloak next to the door and a single clay bowl and wooden spoon.

We left the hut and made our way quietly around the back, to where the thin column of smoke was rising. Next to her garden was a large and very rusty iron cauldron fixed above a fire with a ladle hanging next to it. Most households had such a vessel for cooking and washing clothes. It smelled as if Pelagia was cooking some kind of stew. She must have left it there to simmer while she went into the woods to gather herbs. I decided it was best for us to wait for her in front of her hut so as not to startle her when she returned. But I thought maybe I should first stir the stew for her to make sure it wasn't scalding on the bottom. And so I lifted off the lid.

There were large chunks of cooked meat floating on the top, as was normal enough, but the smell was strange. There were also far too many bones, as if someone had dismembered a large calf and put the entire animal into the pot. I carefully eased the ladle to the bottom and hit something large and hard. I worked the ladle underneath it and pulled it to the top. It was a human skull.

I screamed and fell backward onto the ground.

"Deirdre, what is it?" Dari said.

I could barely talk. "Dari—the stew—it's Pelagia!"

She stood speechless for a moment, then moved toward the pot. I jumped up and ran in front of her.

"No! Kevin, please take her back across the bridge. Dari, I don't want you to see this."

"Deirdre," she almost whispered, "do you mean someone killed Pelagia and put her in the cauldron to cook?"

"Yes. Please, Dari, let me deal with this. I need to examine what's left of the body and I don't want you to watch. We can't carry this cauldron back to the monastery. I've got to look at it here."

It was then that I remembered why Dari was my best friend. In spite of the fact that she was shaking and clearly ready to faint, she forced herself to face me and spoke with a clear, strong voice.

"Deirdre, Sister Anna sent me to take care of Pelagia and that's exactly what I mean to do. You may help me if you wish. In fact, I'd be grateful if you would."

We put out the fire, then I took off my bardic robes and laid them on top of a nearby juniper bush. I went inside the hut to fetch the blanket from on top of the sleeping mat and spread it on the ground next to the cauldron. When this was done, I helped Kevin and Dari pour the contents slowly on top of it.

Pieces of flesh and parts of bones came spilling out and settled on the blanket, while most of the broth drained away across the small yard into the lake. Even with all the experience I had helping Father Ailbe with surgeries and amputations, not to mention the autopsies of the last week, nothing prepared me for this examination.

I couldn't help but gag as I sorted through the remains. There was nothing left that was recognizably human except for her skull. The other bones had been crushed into small pieces. There were knife marks on the leg and arm bones indicating that the flesh had been scraped away. Pelagia hadn't simply been killed, she had been butchered. All the flesh had been thoroughly cooked. The cauldron must have been above the fire for hours.

When we had finished, we walked to the water to wash, then the three of us went in front of the hut to talk. Kevin looked so shaken that I was afraid he was going to fall down, so I suggested we sit on the grass.

"Deirdre," Dari said at last, "please don't tell me this is some kind of sacrifice performed in the old days."

I couldn't even look her in the eyes as I spoke.

"I can tell you this much. In ancient times, on rare occasions, there was a sacrifice of human flesh to the three mother goddesses of the earth, the givers of life. The victim was always an older woman of the tribe, a volunteer, who gave her body as an offering for her people. The druids would kill her painlessly, then dismember her flesh to cook in a cauldron. When it was finished, it was placed into the earth as an offering to the goddesses. But such a thing hasn't been done for many centuries."

"Does that mean the killer is coming back?" Kevin asked. "Maybe we could wait here and catch him."

"I don't think so. He would see that the fire was out anyway and know that someone had been here. He wouldn't approach the crannog now. He may have wanted us to find her like this anyway, just to make it more horrible for everyone."

Dari shuddered and looked at me.

"You keep saying 'he'—but how do you know it isn't a woman doing all this? Do you think women aren't capable of such cruelty?"

"No, it's not because of that. I've known women in my life who could be as vicious as any man, but I don't think that's the case with these murders. There are many female druids, but few are trained sacrificers. It's just not a specialty that attracts many women."

"But you said every druid receives the training to perform these rituals. Why would it have to be a sacrificer?"

"It wouldn't necessarily, but these murders show a detailed knowledge of anatomy and working with flesh. I could be wrong, but I think whoever is doing them is either a sacrificer or has a lot of experience butchering animals."

"What about those two fishermen?" Kevin asked. "Could they have done this?"

"I don't see how," I said. "They're not druids and they probably haven't slaughtered anything bigger than a salmon. Besides, they aren't the type who would commit murder."

"Are you sure you could recognize the type of person who would?" asked Dari.

I sighed and looked at the remains of Pelagia on the blanket.

"Maybe not."

We sat quietly for a few minutes, listening to the birds singing in the trees beyond the pond.

"Deirdre," Dari asked at last, "should we bury her here, or take what's left of her body back to Kildare?"

"Normally I would say we should take her remains back to the cemetery, but I don't think that's practical in this case."

"Then let's just take her skull," she said. "There should be something of her to bury beneath a cross in our cemetery."

We all agreed; so while Kevin dug a hole in back of the house, Dari took the skull from the top of the blanket and wrapped it gently inside her new veil. We then raised the blanket from the corners, tied them together in the center, and carefully lowered the bundle into the hole. Kevin filled it in and we stood together to say a short prayer.

Dari went back inside the hut and brought out both the cross on the wall and the pearls. She placed them along with the skull in her satchel, and then we walked back across the bridge down the road that led to Kildare.

No one spoke a word on the whole journey back.

It was becoming dark when we finally reached the front gate of the monastery. Sister Anna was standing next to it with two of the king's guards. I presumed she was giving them instructions to go and search for Dari and Kevin when she saw us coming. I stopped at the edge of the woods about a hundred feet from the gate. Dari looked back at me, then walked on to Sister Anna. I stood there as I saw her talking with the abbess, who reached out at one point to steady herself on the gatepost.

Dari, Kevin, and the guards went inside the monastery just as the last rays of the sun faded from the western sky. Sister Anna remained there, looking out at me in the distance as I waited. Then she went back inside the monastery grounds and closed the gate behind her.

Chapter Twelve

I spent most of that night thinking about the three murdered sisters. Two of them were from the eastern clans
of my own tribe and of course all three were nuns; but
aside from that, they had had very little in common. The only
other similarity between the three was that Brigid had changed
their lives—though this could be said for many of the nuns.

Grainne was an old woman from a peasant family who had
become a Christian when she met Brigid fifty years earlier after
losing her husband and young daughter to a fever. She had
told me once that she had been on the verge of killing herself
when Brigid came to her small farm and helped her find her
way back to life. Saoirse, on the other hand, was from a wealthy
family of the local warrior nobility who had been raised as

a Christian from childhood. She often said that her earliest memory was sitting in Brigid's lap when she was no more than three years old, listening to our founder as she laughed and told her stories. Pelagia stood apart from the other two as a foreigner and a woman with an almost mystical reputation, among Christians and druids alike. One of the few things I knew about her was a story I had heard from Brigid herself. She said she had met Pelagia even before she founded the monastery, in the early days when she had come to Kildare to try to persuade King Dúnlaing to lease her the land for the monastery. She had seen Pelagia on the road one rainy night and invited her back to her hut. Even though they couldn't speak the same language, Pelagia had somehow communicated that she had been wandering for a long time and wanted to find a place where she could live alone and pray. Brigid had led her to the small crannog and helped her settle there as a solitary.

That was the magic of Brigid. She had the gift of seeing inside everyone she met and giving each what they needed. Sometimes it was nothing more than a kind word or a jar of honey, sometimes it was healing and a new beginning. But if the murderer was targeting victims whose lives Brigid had changed, he would have to kill most of the people in Kildare.

I left my grandmother's house before sunrise and set off down the path back to Finian's farm. About two hours later, I was passing by the short trail that branched off to Cill Fine, the oldest church in Ireland. It had been founded almost a century earlier by Palladius, the first bishop in Ireland. Palladius was a member of the Gaulish nobility who had served Pope Celestine as a deacon and church diplomat on missions to his homeland and Britain. Celestine ordained him and sent him to the south of Ireland when he received word that there were Christian slaves captured from Britain on our island. Palladius had limited success in persuading Irish slave-owners to let him minister to their property, but he did found several churches over the years he worked in Leinster. Cell Fine was the only one still standing. Inside the church was the tomb of Palladius and an altar with relics of Peter and Paul brought from Rome. The churchmen at Armagh were always embarrassed by the fact that Palladius had arrived in Ireland long before their patron Patrick. They tried to minimize his contribution and claimed he had left in disgrace after only a year or two, but everyone in our province knew better. My grandmother remembered meeting him when she was a little girl and said he was a kindly old man dedicated to good works.

The old church was no longer used for services, but one of our solitaries, Sister Fedelm, had moved there years ago as a caretaker and lived in it as her hermitage. She was another of the nuns from the eastern clans of our tribe, but I wasn't worried about her safety since she had returned to the monastery immediately after Sister Anna's order. I liked Fedelm, but she was one of the most nervous people I had ever met. One Sunday when she was back at the monastery for services, a small mouse ran across the floor in front of us on the sisters' side of the church as we knelt in prayer. She ran screaming from the room just as Father Ailbe was blessing the wine for the Eucharist, almost making him drop the chalice.

As I passed the Cill Fine trail, a man came stumbling toward me from the direction of the church. He was bleeding from a wound behind his ear. I recognized him at once as Brother Michael, our new monk from Gaul. I ran to him just as he collapsed onto the ground.

"Michael, what happened? What are you doing here?"

He was moaning and incoherent, so I gave him some water and held him up against myself to drink it.

"Please, try to tell me."

He recognized me at last and grabbed my robe with his hand as he began shouting something incomprehensible at me in his native language. He was still trying to learn Irish.

"Michael, I don't speak Gaulish! Tell me in Latin."

He nodded.

"Deirdre," he said slowly. "We came back for the relics. Fedelm forgot to take them when she left. She was worried about them. I was her guard . . . her guard."

"Where is Fedelm?" I demanded.

"In the church," he said. "I didn't see him. He hit me from behind. I blacked out. I couldn't help her. Holy God, Deirdre. I swear, I couldn't help her."

I left him lying in the grass and started to run down the trail to the church.

When I got there, the door was open. I drew my sword and rushed inside—but I knew I would be too late. The fourth sacrifice was to Crom Crúach, the darkest of Irish gods. Some Christians called him Lucifer, the devil, but he was nothing like the biblical angel of light who fell from heaven. Crom Crúach was primordial chaos, the embodiment of the madness that always threatens to tear our world apart. Few Irish actually worshiped him, but the druids taught that neither could we ignore him. Even darkness has its place in the balance of the universe.

Fedelm was stretched out on her back on top of the altar in the front of the small church. Her tunic had been torn from her. Her arms and legs were tied firmly to the bottom of the altar. She was cut open in a single deep incision from the base of her throat to her lower belly. Fedelm's heart rested on the altar next to her. Her face was frozen in horror. Victims dedicated to Crom Crúach were not given mistletoe to drink, and they were never volunteers. It was an essential part of this darkest of sacrificial rituals that they be innocents, usually slaves, taken unaware and tied to an altar against their will. They would be forced to watch, still alive, as they were slit open and their beating heart pulled from their body.

I closed her eyes. Her skin was still warm to the touch. The murder couldn't have happened more than a half hour earlier. I rushed out the door and ran around the church, looking for the tracks of the killer, but there was nothing.

"Why are you doing this?" I shouted as loudly as I could, shaking with rage, hoping the man could still hear me.

There was only silence.

I went back to the road and found Brother Michael sitting against a tree, weeping with his face in his hands. I quickly examined his head and could see that the place where he had been struck was swelling, but that he was in no danger. I forced him to his feet and marched him back down the trail to the church. I brought an old cart out of the barn and rolled it next to the front door of the church. Michael refused to go back inside, so I went in, untied Fedelm's body, and wrapped it in a blanket from her bed by myself, first placing her heart back inside her chest. I then carried her in my arms out the door to the cart and laid her gently inside. There were no animals to draw the small wagon, so I put on the yoke and began pulling it down the path to Kildare, Michael trailing behind me.

Chapter Thirteen

The horror of what I had seen that day and the days before was beginning to take its toll on me. I couldn't eat and didn't dare sleep, for fear that what I had seen would return in my dreams. So I spent most of that same night sitting with my grandmother in her hut, talking about what had happened and what I should do next. She agreed that Finian was a prime suspect in all four murders, but that we had no proof of his guilt. We talked about asking the king to arrest him immediately, but we knew this would be a gross violation of Irish law. It was a fundamental principle of the legal traditions of our people that no man or woman could be deprived of their freedom without evidence, preferably in the form of sworn testimony from a person of high status.

I heard early the next morning that Sister Anna had sent one of the guards to the king during the night to report on the latest killing. The man was back by dawn with ten more warriors and orders from the king to bring the remaining nuns back to the monastery whether they wanted to come or not. I decided to go to my cousin Riona immediately in hope of avoiding a scene between her and the king's men. I knew she wouldn't go with them willingly and I didn't want to see her dragged from her home by force.

I strapped my sword to my belt, took a large staff from the corner of the hut, and headed down the path just as it was getting light. A heavy rain was falling, making the track through the woods a muddy mess.

I knew a farmer not far from the monastery who raised sheep, and I was sure he would take Riona's small flock until all this was over. With the help of her dogs, we could have them there by noon and Riona safely within the monastery walls by dinner. The problem was what to do with her dogs. Sister Anna would never allow five fierce sheepdogs inside the monastery grounds, but I knew they would be uncontrollable away from Riona.

I readied my staff as I approached her farm in case the dogs reached me before Riona did. I didn't think they would attack me if I stood still and didn't try to come closer to the house, but I wasn't sure. I stopped at the edge of the meadow, well away from her hermitage, and made certain I was standing next to a tall tree with low branches in case I needed to climb it quickly. Then I called out for her and waited. I could see that the sheep were still in their pen, which was strange for so late in the morning. I called again and prepared to be rushed by a pack of angry hounds, but there was no sound. I moved out of the woods slowly and approached the house, calling out several more times in case she and the dogs were in the back garden or down by the stream.

Next to a large elm tree midway between the meadow and the yard, I saw a pool of blood on the ground with trails of dark red leading toward the house. Behind the tree, the trails ended with the bodies of five dogs riddled with arrows. I drew my sword and called out for Riona frantically. I heard a crash in the house and ran to the open front door. Riona was lying on the floor inside.

She had a noose around her neck but was conscious and struggling to sit up. I rushed to her side and held her up as I worked the flax rope off her neck. It had dug deeply into her skin and was tightly fixed from behind, but I managed to get it over her head. She had cuts on her face and hands as if she had been in a fight. There were broken dishes on the floor, and a large jar was smashed against the fireplace. I brought her a cup of water and waited until she was at last able to speak in a rasping voice.

"Deirdre—he must have heard you coming—he came up from behind—when I was by the fire—my dogs—where are they?"

"Out by the elm tree. I'm so sorry, Riona, but they're dead. Someone shot them with arrows."

She tried to get up and go to the door but fell back down.

"Wait. You're in no shape to move. Just rest here. I've got my sword. He won't be coming back."

She sat for a few minutes, trying with great effort to breathe. The rope must have bruised her windpipe. I bound the wounds on her hands and wiped the blood off her face with a rag.

"Did you see who it was? Did you recognize him?" I asked. She nodded and took another sip of water.

"He had a hood on—black—but I fought him—pulled it off."

"Who was it?"

She grimaced from the pain of speaking, but continued.

"It was him—the bastard—he killed my dogs."

"Who? Who was it?"

"Finian."

Chapter Fourteen

I tried to get Riona to rest, but she insisted on leaving the house to see her dogs. She knelt beside them and wept. I put my arm around her.

"We don't have time to bury them now," I said. "I've got to get word to the king to arrest Finian before he disappears. Are you strong enough to make it to Grandmother's house?"

"Yes."

I covered the dogs with a tarp to keep the crows away. I would send someone back to take care of the sheep. I led Riona slowly down the path, supporting her as we walked through the pouring rain and keeping both eyes open for Finian in case he tried to ambush us. It took us almost an hour to reach my grandmother's home. She was in the garden when we arrived.

I explained to her quickly what had happened and helped her get Riona settled on a bed inside. Then I ran down the road to the monastery as fast as I could. Kevin was at the gate talking with several of the guards. I told them everything that had happened. The leader sent a rider to the king almost before I had finished speaking. He sent another three of his men on horseback to Riona's farm to pick up Finian's trail if they could find it. With all the rain, I had my doubts. Then, leaving a handful of guards at the monastery, he galloped off with four others to Finian's farm.

"Do you want to come in and tell Sister Anna?" Kevin asked.

"No, please, you do it. I've got to get back to my grandmother's house to check on Riona. I know the king will want to see her as soon as possible."

I asked one of the remaining guards for a horse, since I knew Riona wasn't fit to walk. The man hesitated, but I was in no mood for delays. I threw my bardic cloak around me with a flourish and fixed him with my eyes. He was holding his own horse for me a minute later as I mounted it and bolted down the trail to Grandmother's house. By the time I got there, Riona was sitting up by the fire.

"Riona, are you fit to ride to the king? I hate to ask you to do it, but he'll want to see you right away. He needs to hear what happened directly from you, to make the testimony valid."

In Irish law, nuns and monks were considered equal in status to druids. As witnesses, they were outranked only by a king. The fact that Riona's father had been a respected warrior made her testimony even stronger.

"Yes, I'm feeling better now," she said. "But you should ride double, behind me, so you can steady me if I need it."

We set off down the road at a fast canter. We stopped twice so she could rest and drink some water, but by early afternoon we were at the king's feasting hall.

Dúnlaing was waiting there, surrounded by several of his most trusted warriors, including Saoirse's father. He placed Riona in his own chair and called for a slave to bring her a cup of wine. She was exhausted from the ride and her voice was still hoarse from the rope, but she drank the wine gladly and said she was ready to talk.

"Riona, daughter of Oisín, do you swear to speak only the truth before your king and these witnesses?"

"I do, my lord."

"Who was it who tried to kill you this morning?"

"It was Finian, the druid sacrificer."

"Is there any doubt in your mind that it was Finian?"

"None, my lord."

"Was there anyone else with him?"

"Not that I saw."

"And you make this testimony knowing that to speak falsely before your king brings a sentence of death on your head?"

"Yes, my lord."

"I'll have one of my servants take you to my guest house and watch after you."

"Thank you, my king."

He clapped his hands and an old woman appeared to lead Riona away. The king then bade his men and me to sit at the table. A slave brought each of us a cup of wine.

"Thank the gods this is over," the king said.

"Only if we can catch Finian," Saoirse's father said.

"We'll catch him. Besides the men out looking for him, I've posted guards on all the border roads and sent word to the neighboring kings to hold him if he comes to their lands. They won't risk war by defying me. No one would protect a murderer in any case."

He turned to me.

"Deirdre, it goes without saying that I expect the full cooperation of the Druid Order in this matter."

"Of course, my lord. We would never harbor such a fugitive. Finian has brought shame on all of us."

The king then talked with us for an hour or more, asking our advice on how best to restore calm and order to the kingdom. He was insistent that there was to be no retribution against the druids after Finian was punished. He wanted the matter to end there. He looked at Saoirse's father as he said this, and the man finally nodded his head in agreement. Dúnlaing spoke of the need for cooperation between people of different faiths and pledged to help the monastery of Brigid recover.

We heard horses approaching from outside the feasting hall and rose from our chairs. The lead guard from the monastery and his men marched into the hall with Finian held in chains between them. His face was covered with bruises, but he wore a look of pure defiance.

"He was at his farm, my lord. The fool didn't even try to run—though he wasn't cooperative."

The king took his place on his chair at the front of the hall and ordered Finian brought before him. Saoirse's father stood near, fingering his sword.

"Finian, son of Esras, you stand here accused of the murder of four women, sisters of the monastery of Brigid. What say you?"

Finian spat blood onto the ground along with two of his teeth, but said nothing.

"You understand," said the king, "that silence will be taken as an admission of guilt?"

Finian stood there, saying not a word.

"So be it," said Dúnlaing. "You are sentenced to die for your crimes. Take him into the yard."

The men led Finian out of the hall. Saoirse's father approached the king and spoke.

"My lord, let me do it. This man killed my daughter and defiled her body. I claim the right to end this man's life. I want to hold his bloody head in my hands after I sever it from his neck."

The king put his hand on the man's shoulder.

"My old friend, normally I would be glad to let you deal with this criminal, but that would be too quick a punishment in this case. Come with me into the yard. I have something better planned."

We followed Dúnlaing into the large space in front of the feasting hut. I saw that a small crowd had assembled near a tall wooden post that was being stacked around with dry kindling. When all was in place, the king spoke.

"Bind him to the stake."

The men pushed Finian forward and fixed his hands behind the pole with iron chains. As much as I despised Finian at that moment, I couldn't help but admire his courage. Burning was not a common form of execution in our land. It was slow and horrifically painful and reserved only for the most heinous of crimes. Yet Finian stood tall, gazing up to the heavens with a look of calm determination on his face.

"Do you have any last words, druid?" the king asked.

Finian said nothing.

"Light the fire," Dúnlaing said.

The king's men brought blazing torches and placed them at the edges of the pyre. Sometimes kings would pour oil on a pyre to make it burn faster and hasten the death of a victim. Sometimes they would use water once the fire had caught hold, to make dense smoke and suffocate the condemned man before the flames reached him. Dúnlaing did neither.

I watched as the flames worked their way slowly to the center of the pyre. When they reached Finian, I expected him to scream in pain as his clothes caught fire and his flesh was seared. But in spite of the indescribable agony he must have felt, he uttered not a sound. In the last moments before his body was engulfed in the fire, he turned his head to look at me with an expression of pure hatred. And then he was gone.

Chapter Fifteen

It was almost a week after the death of Finian before I could sleep through the night again. The images of his execution and the murders of the nuns kept jarring me awake at all hours. But life was beginning to return to normal, though the scars remained for us all.

I was still expelled from my life at the monastery, of course. Just because the killer had been caught didn't mean Sister Anna was going to change her mind. I didn't really blame her. She had told me that I had to choose where my loyalties lay—and I had. But what would I do now?

The king's guards left the monastery, and the solitaries returned to their hermitages. Riona had recovered nicely from her ordeal. A shepherd had given her three adorable sheepdog puppies, and she was busy training them at her farm. Parents were no longer afraid to send their children to school, so Dari and the rest of the teachers were busy again with classes. The only visible sign of the horrors of those few days were four new crosses above four freshly dug graves in the monastery cemetery just outside the walls of Kildare.

A few days later, I was happy to see Father Ailbe walking down the path to my grandmother's house with two fishing poles in his hands. I ran out the door and gave him such a hug that I almost knocked him over.

"Abba, it's so good to see you. How have you been?"

"Fine, my child. It's wonderful to see you again, as well. Those robes look very impressive on you."

I twirled around like a girl showing off a new outfit for a festival.

"Thank you. I'm trying to get used to them again."

Father Ailbe was my teacher and mentor from my earliest memory. Not having a father or grandfather of my own, he was both to me, and much more. He believed in me when few others did and was always on my side. He urged me to question tradition and try new things, though it sometimes got me into trouble.

I remember when I was ten years old, sitting in druidic school one day, listening to an Irish story about warriors fighting over the best cut of meat from a pig, I began to wonder why we wrote down only Latin texts at the monastery. Hadn't anyone ever tried to write in Irish? When I got back home that evening, I took out my wax tablet and began to write in Roman letters the beginning of the Irish tale I had heard from the bard that day:

> There was a famous king of the Leinstermen.
> His name was Mac Dathó.

I was surprised at how well this worked. By bedtime, I had managed to write out the whole story of Mac Dathó's pig in Irish on a piece of old parchment.

I was so proud of myself that I showed my work to the chief druid the next day at school. He was horrified and ripped the parchment to pieces in front of the class. He then lectured me on the evil of trying to capture the matchless beauty of Irish stories in the scribbling of the Christians. We were oral poets, he proudly declared, wagging his finger in my face. If we began to write down our tales, our memories would become as useless as a fat stallion at a horse race. When he was done shaming me, I returned to my bench in tears while the class snickered.

But when I told Father Ailbe, he said that writing in Irish was a wonderful idea. He said a monk named Mesrob had done the same thing with Armenian a century earlier for his Bible translation. He told me that there would be great challenges in devising a system for written Irish, but that I could do it if anyone could. After that day, I began to experiment and refine my Irish alphabet, though I didn't dare tell any of the bards what I was doing. I doubted my Irish alphabet would ever become widespread, but it was just the sort of project Father Ailbe was always encouraging me to pursue.

"So, Abba, are we going fishing?"

Father Ailbe loved to fish. Ever since I'd been a little girl, I would go with him to the stream flowing through the trees behind the monastery and fish for trout. He would always catch a basketful and bring them back to the sisters for supper. He was never so happy as when he held a fishing pole in his hand.

We walked back down the path to our favorite fishing spot. We sat down by the stream and baited our hooks, then cast them into the water.

"Did I ever tell you about the time I went fishing for crocodiles in the Nile?" he asked.

"No, Abba. Tell me."

"It wasn't exactly fishing, I suppose, though we did use bait of a sort. I went with some villagers near Elephantine in the far south one autumn just after the annual flood had subsided. I had traveled upriver to arrange a grain deal for my father and had struck up a friendship with some of the peasants I met there. Downstream in Thebes, they still worshiped crocodiles and mummified their bodies. But the people of Elephantine had no such scruples. For them, it was a grand adventure and a chance for fresh meat."

"How big were these crocodiles?" I asked.

"Well, Herodotus says they grow to more than twenty-five feet, but you can't believe anything he writes. Still, a few of the adult males I saw were at least eighteen feet long from nose to tail. They are fast and ferociously strong. I once saw one grab a farmer who had gone down to the river bank to gather papyrus reeds. The creature practically exploded from its hiding place in the water and had the poor man by the legs before he could even scream. It quickly pulled him back into the river and began to roll over and over. The farmer tried to grab its jaws and pull them apart, but it was no use. A single child can hold a crocodile's jaws shut, but it would take a dozen strong men to pry them open. His friends just stood watching in horror, knowing there was nothing they could do."

I shuddered at the thought. The most dangerous thing you could find in an Irish river was an ill-tempered otter.

"On the night we went fishing, the villagers took along two small pigs and a length of sturdy rope with a large hook on the end. When we got to the river's edge, they slaughtered one of the pigs and ran the hook through its back. Then they threw the bloody carcass into the river.

"I had supposed the other pig was spare bait, so I was surprised when they began to beat on the animal with a stick. Its squeals were so loud, they echoed across the river. I was about to demand that they stop this cruel behavior when one of them pointed to the middle of the stream. A large crocodile had appeared, swimming toward the carcass of the dead pig. I realized then that they had used the noise made by the live animal to attract the attention of the crocodile—and it worked. The jaws closed on the bait and it began its death-roll, only to find that it had a hook stuck in its throat. The crocodile roared in pain and anger, but the sharp point was fixed deep in its gullet. When it had at last exhausted itself, the villagers pulled it to shore with the rope and quickly covered its eyes with mud. Once blinded, it was easy to kill."

I always enjoyed Father Ailbe's stories. We then sat in silence for a long time waiting for the fish to bite.

"Abba, can I ask you a question?"

"Of course."

"Do you think a person can be both a druid and a Christian?"

He was quiet for a minute, moving his line to lure a trout he had seen hiding beneath the opposite bank.

"I suppose it depends on what you mean. There are many druid teachings such as the dignity of the individual, compassion for the poor, and an emphasis on others rather than oneself that are very similar to the teachings of the Gospel. In some areas, such as a respect for the sanctity of nature, I would say that druids are well ahead of Christians. But if you're talking about strict theology, there is no place for a single God, the incarnation of Christ, or heaven as we know it in druid teachings."

"Abba, I believe in Christianity, but I'm not sure it has to be the only religion. Couldn't God have appeared as a man in Palestine five hundred years ago to make his teachings known, but also speak to other people at other times and places in different ways? I mean, what about the untold generations of humanity that lived before Christ was born or those who live now still beyond the reach of Christian missionaries? Are they doomed to hell because they were born in the wrong time or place?"

Father Ailbe was having no luck persuading the trout to come out of its hiding place. He slowly moved his line back to our side of the stream.

"I think, Deirdre, that there is too much talk about eternal punishment in Christian circles. Jesus hardly ever mentions it in his sermons. He was much more concerned about how we live this life. Now, I believe in an afterlife, and it's very possible that some of us may have to do some more suffering before we're ready for heaven, but the current Christian preoccupation with fire and brimstone isn't helpful. I prefer to try to love God and my neighbor as best I can. I'll leave heaven and hell in the hands of one greater than myself."

"I agree with you, Abba, but I guess I'm talking more about my own life than I am theology. Sister Anna says I should choose between being a Christian and a druid. When I talked to Finian, he said I was the worst kind of hypocrite, trying to be two things at once. So I've got both Christians and druids saying I'm a fool. What do you think?"

He looked out at the stream again.

"You're trying too hard, Deirdre."

"But I've got to know the truth."

"No, I mean you're pulling too hard on the line. You'll never catch a fish that way. You need to give it some slack."

I loosened my grip and waited.

"I think, Deirdre, that you remind me of a man I met once in Persia. He was a Zoroastrian priest from a long line of their clergy, but he had been impressed by the teachings of the church and been baptized as a Christian. He tried to carry out his priestly duties every day, offering prayers before the sacred fire of Ahura Mazda and singing the Gatha hymns at holy rituals. Then he would go to church, where he served as a deacon, reciting the creed every Sunday and faithfully receiving the Eucharist."

"What happened to him?"

"I heard that a few months after I left, he was stoned to death as a heretic by both the Zoroastrians and Christians."

My eyes grew wide.

"Abba, that's horrible. Do you think that's my fate as well?"

He smiled.

"No, my child. Ireland is a much more tolerant land than Persia. I think you'll live a long and happy life here as both a druid and a Christian. But I don't think it will be easy for you."

Just then, the trout he had been wooing swam across from the opposite bank and took the bait. He played the fish until it was exhausted, then pulled it out of the water with a single flick of his wrist and removed the hook from its mouth.

"Fresh fish for dinner," he said. "But I need to catch a few more."

"Abba, assuming I can walk this line between two worlds without falling on my face, what should I do about being a nun?"

He baited another line.

"Do you really want to be a nun, Deirdre?"

"I think so. The monastery was a refuge for me after my son died. I was lost and didn't know where else to go. After that, I decided that being a nun was something I truly wanted to do. I saw it as a way to serve God and fight for the vision of Brigid on this island. And after the events of the last few weeks, I think Kildare needs nuns more than ever. I don't mean just to replace the four we lost, but as a statement to the world that the work of the monastery is important. But Sister Anna quite publicly expelled me from the community. She's not the sort of person who changes her mind."

"That is true," he said. "Would you like me to talk with her?"

"Maybe not yet. I think I should let things settle down a little more at the monastery. And I have to admit, I like wearing these robes."

"They do bring out the blue in your eyes."

I laughed and moved my line yet again. I was having no luck at all in catching anything.

"Deirdre, are you there?"

Dari was coming up the path behind us.

"Over here, Dari. Do you want to take over my pole? You can't help but do better than me today."

"No, thanks. Sister Anna sent me out to look for Alma. I'm horrible at fishing, anyway."

Sister Alma was a nun in her mid-forties from King Dúnlaing's own clan. She was the monastery librarian and also an excellent scribe with perpetually ink-stained fingers who spent most of her time copying texts in our scriptorium.

"Where was Alma going?"

"She left four days ago to visit her parents on their farm over by the Liffey. They were terribly worried about her the last couple of weeks, and you know they're too feeble to travel anymore, so she went for a quick visit. She was supposed to be back last evening."

"She probably just decided to stay at the farm an extra day," I said.

"I know, but Sister Anna has been insistent about everyone returning from trips on time. Alma is going to get an earful from the abbess when she gets back."

"I'll help you look. I'm not doing anything useful here, anyway. Do you mind, Abba?"

"No, please go ahead. I think I'll head back to the monastery myself. The fish just aren't biting today."

Father Ailbe walked slowly back down the path to Kildare with his single fish tied to a line over his shoulder.

"Let's get started, Dari. The longer it takes to find Alma, the more trouble she's going to be in with Sister Anna."

Chapter Sixteen

By evening, I was starting to get worried. Dari and I had walked all the way to the farm of Alma's parents and back. They said she had left to return to Kildare after breakfast the day before. Her mother was beside herself with fear after all that had happened over the last two weeks, but I assured her that the killer had been caught and there was no longer any danger to the nuns. Dari had reported the news to Sister Anna, and the abbess had sent out search parties to comb the countryside between Kildare and the Liffey. She was thinking of asking the king for help but didn't want to take that step yet. Alma was notorious for living in her own world. We would often find her at the scriptorium in the mornings, copying some manuscript, not even knowing the night had passed. One time when she was supposed to be meeting with some visiting dignitaries from Britain, I found her sitting in a tree drawing pictures of baby birds to use in a book illustration. She had likely wandered off to visit a friend or a favorite meadow on the way home and forgotten that she was supposed to return right away to Kildare.

I found Dari outside the monastery gate talking with two of the monks about where to look next. Brother Fiach was about to set off down the little-used path that ran to the Liffey north of Kildare in case Alma had decided to return that way. Brother Michael, his head still bandaged, volunteered to search in the forest to the south in case she had somehow become lost there.

"Deirdre, I don't like this," Dari said after they left. "It's hardly been a week since Finian was executed and now we have another missing nun. People were just starting to feel safe again, but this has put everyone on edge."

"I understand, but you know Alma. Remember when last year she disappeared for three days before anyone could find her?"

"Yes. She was on the far side of Dunmurry Hill, collecting oak apples to make ink."

"Don't worry, she'll turn up. But I hope Sister Anna gives her a good tongue-lashing when she does, for worrying everyone so much."

We strolled away from the gate down to the edge of the woods.

"Deirdre, have you thought about asking Sister Anna if you could return to the monastery? I really miss you."

"I miss you too. Father Ailbe talked with me about the same thing this morning. He offered to speak with her."

"You should let him. How can she refuse Father Ailbe?"

"She can do anything she wants. The abbess is in charge of the nuns, not him. I know he has a lot of influence with her;

but if she's made up her mind, she's not going to change it, even for him."

We wandered toward the graveyard as we talked.

"Well, I don't see the problem," Dari said. "The crisis is over. Everyone said things they didn't mean. Couldn't you just swallow your pride and apologize to her?"

"It's not a matter of pride, I. . . ."

I stopped and stared at the far side of the graveyard.

"Dari, why am I seeing *five* new crosses?"

"Five? What do you mean? There were only four nuns buried recently."

We started to walk faster. The sun had set and it was growing dark, but it was clear that there were five new graves, the last with *very* fresh earth. I knelt down quickly to look at the cross in the dim light. There was no name inscribed on it, just a small circle with two diagonal lines coming from the top.

"Dari, dig fast!"

I threw off my robes and began to dig at the earth frantically with my hands. Dari realized what was happening and joined in with all her might.

"There's a shovel in the shed," she gasped.

"Get it quickly. Help! Anybody, help!" I shouted toward the monastery.

Dari ran to the shed and returned in a moment with the wooden shovel. She was small but strong and threw the loose earth behind her as fast as any man.

Kevin came running down the hill and didn't even ask what we were doing. He took one look at the fifth grave and tore into it with his hands, then took the shovel from Dari when she tired. Others rushed to the site, but there wasn't room for anyone else to dig. Dari and I, covered in dirt, collapsed at the side while two others took our places. We had dug down five feet in just a few minutes and still had found nothing. Sister

Anna and Father Ailbe hurried down the hill as well and stood by the grave as the younger members of the community continued to dig frantically.

Finally Kevin struck something, and I jumped in. I pushed the dirt away and saw that it was a cloth shroud.

"Kevin, help me!"

I lifted the head and front of the body as he grabbed the feet. We pushed it up out of the grave, into the arms of the nuns and brothers waiting there, who laid it gently on the earth. Father Ailbe took the knife he always carried for woodcarving and cut away the coverings at the head to reveal the face of a woman.

It was Sister Alma.

He placed his hands on her neck to feel for a pulse, but shook his head. I knelt next to him and felt her skin. It was cold to the touch.

"She has been dead for many hours," Father Ailbe said to Sister Anna and the rest of us.

Alma had the same look of peace on her face as most of the other murdered nuns.

Sister Anna took charge quickly.

"Kevin, you and the other brothers choose a sister and go in pairs to the hermitages of the solitaries. Each of you, man and woman, take a sword or a spear. Bring the solitaries back here immediately, even if you have to carry them kicking and screaming. I will send word to the king right away. Some of you carry Sister Alma's body to the infirmary. The rest, return to the monastery and form a guard until the king's men arrive. Go, now!"

Everyone went to work immediately. Four of the sisters, Dari among them, took up Alma's body and carried it to the infirmary, with Father Ailbe walking beside them. I didn't need to hear the autopsy results. I knew he would find that she had been rendered unconscious with mistletoe and buried alive, a sacrifice to Donn, the god of death.

Only Sister Anna and I remained by the grave.

"The sign carved on the cross, Sister Anna, it's the same as the one carved on Saoirse's chest."

"I can see that."

I started to cry, something I had never done before in the presence of the abbess. She made no move to comfort me.

"I'm so sorry, Sister Anna. I thought it was all over. I thought we had caught the killer."

"I had thought so as well. It seems as if there was more than one. Or perhaps someone new has been inspired to continue Finian's work."

"I'll find him, Sister Anna. The king's commission to me still holds. I won't let you down."

She looked directly at me for the first time.

"I hope so, Deirdre, I truly do. Alma was a member of the king's own clan, a cousin on his father's side, I believe. If things were bad with the previous four killings, they are about to get much worse. A storm is coming—and I don't know who, whether druid or Christian, will be left alive when it's over."

Chapter Seventeen

We received word the next morning that King Dúnlaing had called an assembly of all the clan and religious leaders of the tribe at his feasting hall that evening.

The king's guards had returned to Kildare in even greater numbers than before. All the solitaries had been gathered inside the monastery grounds. Sister Anna had not been exaggerating when she said they were to be brought in even against their will. Sister Maria, a white-haired nun from Britain who lived west of the monastery, was forcibly carried through the gates by one of the king's men, who had a black eye from struggling with her. My cousin Riona had reluctantly left her new puppies and sheep with a nearby farmer and made a bed for herself in the loft above the cattle barn.

My grandmother and I met Father Ailbe making his way down the road to the king's farm. Sister Anna had gone ahead on horseback, accompanied by two of Dúnlaing's guards.

"Abba," I said as I took his satchel and put it on my shoulder, "why didn't you ride with Sister Anna? I'm sure the king would have found a horse for you or sent a chariot."

"I'm sure he would have, but my knee is feeling better. A little exercise is just the thing to loosen up the joints. Besides, I find that walking and thinking go together very nicely."

"Will it bother you if we join you, Ailbe?" asked Grandmother.

"Not at all. I can think even better if I have someone to talk with. Is there any word from Cathbad?"

Cathbad was a druid prophet who lived near the old royal settlement of Cruachu in Connacht beyond the Shannon River. If my grandmother was the leading druid in the province of Leinster, Cathbad was the acknowledged senior druid over all of Ireland. There was no official hierarchy in the Order, but he had been the most respected and influential druid on the island since I was a little girl.

"Yes," she said, "he sent a message that he was on his way here as fast as possible. I'm hoping he arrives in time for the king's assembly. If anyone can keep things under control, it's Cathbad."

"Is it true," Father Ailbe asked, "that several of the western clans are calling their warriors to arms?"

"Yes," she said. "I heard just a few hours ago that Brion, who holds the king's borderlands along the Barrow River, is assembling his men. He's always prided himself on his support for the druids, many of whom are members of his clan. He has at least thirty skilled warriors at his command and holds great influence with the other western clan leaders. Brion has always resented Dúnlaing. He has made no secret of his belief that the kingship should have passed to his family. He may well see this latest murder as an opportunity to weaken, if not replace, the king."

"And to make matters worse," I said, "Saoirse's father and the clans of the east are also arming their men. The king will try to stay impartial, but if it comes to a fight, Dúnlaing will support the eastern clans. Not only have they always been his power base, but many of them are sympathetic to the Christians if not Christians themselves. And the fact that four of the murdered nuns have been from the eastern clans, with Alma from the king's own family, makes it certain that Dúnlaing would side with them."

"Kildare lies in the middle of the kingdom between the eastern and western clans," Grandmother said. "Brion is already upset about the king's guards at the monastery. It hasn't escaped his notice that suddenly—and conveniently, in his mind—a few dozen heavily armed warriors of the eastern clans are stationed so near to him."

"Do you think the king can hold the tribe together?" I asked.

"I don't know," said my grandmother and Father Ailbe at the same time.

We arrived at the king's settlement in the late afternoon. Dúnlaing's guest house was spacious and comfortable, but the leaders had all pitched their own tents outside the walls near the forest, eastern and western clans as far apart as possible. Sister Anna was alone in the guest house, reading, when the three of us arrived. I had hoped she and my grandmother would both apologize for their previous harsh words, but neither would even look at the other.

After dinner, we heard the horn sounding and made our way to the feasting hall. The tables had been put aside and the benches lined up to face the king's chair in the center near the fire. For such a warm day, there was a noticeable chill inside the hall. The eastern clan leaders sat on the right and the western on the left. Each had brought a retinue of warriors. Father Ailbe, Sister Anna, my grandmother, and I took our places in the center between the eastern and western clans. Three other druids sat with us, including Cáma, the interpreter of dreams who had been at dinner with us at my grandmother's house when we received the news of Grainne's death. That seemed like ages ago now.

The king's resident bard, an old man named Tadg who had been one of my teachers, sat near the fire, softly playing his harp. He was blind now and suffered from pain in his joints, but he was still the finest harpist in Ireland. It was customary for a bard to play during assemblies, to calm the volatile spirits of the warriors present. Sometimes it worked.

The king rose from his chair. He looked magnificent in his flowing robes and thick gold torque. Next to him, leaning against his chair, was his sword.

"I have called you all here today to discuss the most serious matter that has faced our kingdom in many years. Most of you have stood beside me in battle against the Uí Néill armies from the north. We have shed blood together and watched our friends die fighting to protect this tribe against its enemies. But today we face not the swords of the Ulstermen but a more dangerous and insidious foe. I speak not of the blasphemers of all things holy who have murdered five nuns from the monastery of Brigid, as evil as those men are, cursed be their heads. I speak of the divisions between clans, between people of different faiths in this kingdom. Nothing would give our enemies more delight than to see us fall upon each other."

He paused to let his gaze sweep the room, then continued.

"I am the *rí*, the king of this tribe. I rule by the will of the gods as I have for the last fifty years. I will not let dissension and discord tear this tribe apart. We will remain one people. Do I make myself clear?"

There was a murmur of assent from the right side of the hall, but a noticeable silence on the left. Brion, the clan leader from the west, rose to face the king.

"My lord, it is true that you rule this tribe, but you are not an emperor over us as the Romans had among themselves in days gone by. The gods have granted you power over this land, but only as long as you are able to maintain order. You know the clans of the east are arming themselves and that their greedy eyes are fixed westward. You have placed your own warriors at Kildare next to lands my family has held for generations. I grieve for the sisters of Brigid whose lives were lost, but I fear you and your allies here on the banks of the Liffey are using this tragedy as a pretext to expand your own power. I tell you, we will not allow it!"

There were shouts of approval from the left of the hall and angry calls from the right. Tadg played even more loudly.

Saoirse's father stood and waited for the uproar to subside before he began.

"Brion, you dare to speak to us of taking advantage of an outrage to strengthen our eastern clans? Was it your daughter who was murdered? Do you think I would use her death to take a few scrawny cattle from your herds? Or perhaps you think the king bribed a druid to bury alive his own kinswoman? I find it strange you paint us as conspirators while it is our own women who are dying. We all know you have craved power over this tribe for years. It seems to me that if anyone is manipulating the murder of the nuns of Kildare, it is you and your western allies."

Both sides jumped to their feet and began shouting at each other even more loudly. I was glad that their swords weren't allowed in assembly halls, but I was afraid these men would tear each other apart with their bare hands.

Father Ailbe rose from his seat next to me and waited silently. At last the noise subsided and the king nodded to him.

"My friends, as you all know, I am a stranger in this land. I came here from Egypt many years ago when some of your fathers were not yet born. You have welcomed me most graciously to your island and accepted me as one of your own. You are truly a remarkable people of honor, strength, and courage."

I marveled at how he was able to hold these violent men with his voice. But then, Father Ailbe had been trained by the finest rhetoric teachers of Alexandria.

"My city was founded eight hundred years ago by Alexander the Great, a name known even in this distant land. Alexandria prospered like no other city before it. We traded with India and distant Cathay, sailed the seas from the African coast to Scandinavia, even here to Ireland, and we grew rich in both gold and knowledge. We welcomed people of all backgrounds and beliefs to our city, be they gentle Hindus or followers of the fierce Germanic gods. Our differences made us stronger and we honored them. But then jealousy and dissension came among us. For many years the people of my city fought among themselves. Christians tortured and slew believers in the old gods, priests at the temple of Serapis urged their members to kill Christians, and everyone slaughtered the Jews. Alexandria was once a shining jewel, with temples and churches and synagogues that surpassed even Rome and Constantinople. The wisdom and heritage of the whole world was preserved in its libraries and museums. But so much of it has been reduced to ashes and rubble. The citizens of my once-great city now live in fear of conquest by the Persians or even the Arab tribes of the desert. They are weak because they fought among themselves."

The hall was silent until a voice spoke from the back.

"Father Ailbe speaks wisely."

We all turned and saw an old druid standing in the doorway. Like many elderly men of the Order, he had a long white beard. The gnarled oak staff he carried was a symbol of authority, but also helped him as he hobbled down the aisle between the two sides of the hall.

"King Dúnlaing, please forgive my tardiness. It is a long ride from Cruachu for someone of my age."

The king arose.

"Welcome, Cathbad. I am grateful that you have come. The floor is yours to speak."

Cathbad walked to the center of the hall and faced us, standing to the right of the king. Everyone in the room stood as he passed, even the Christians.

"Let me begin with an apology," he said. "Sister Anna, on behalf of the druids of this island, I offer my most sincere condolences to the members of the monastery of holy Brigid at Kildare. The men who carried out these horrendous murders are a disgrace to the Order. They have rejected our teachings and used their knowledge of our ways to bring shame on us all. I pronounce them *maillaithe*—cursed—for all eternity."

A visible shudder went through the room. There was no worse fate than to be damned by the most powerful druid in Ireland. Such a curse echoed in birth and rebirth throughout the ages.

"I also pledge to King Dúnlaing and to all of you here the full cooperation of the Order in finding and punishing the man or men who are blaspheming our ancient ways."

There were sounds of assent from the leaders of the western clans and a few from the east.

"Let us live together in peace," Cathbad concluded, "Christians and druids, followers of old and new ways alike. We are all children of the divine, whether you see the power of heaven as one god or many. We are all connected to each other. We must learn that we are one."

The king stood up.

"Thank you, Cathbad. You have given us much to consider. Let me add my pledge that none of us will rest until the killer of these women is punished. We will work together, no matter our religious differences. We will stand together against the forces that would tear us apart. We are one tribe and one people."

The king dismissed us, and the crowd began making their way out the door. But in spite of the words of reconciliation, I couldn't help but notice that the leaders of the feuding clans were still looking at each other with murder in their eyes.

Chapter Eighteen

My grandmother invited Cathbad to stay at her home, since they had much to discuss. He had arrived in a chariot with a driver, so she decided to accompany them back, though it was not a form of transport she enjoyed. They left as soon as the king's assembly was over, even though it was growing dark. Sister Anna rode back to Kildare as well that same evening, with her two guards. I was happy to spend the night in the king's guest quarters with Father Ailbe and walk back to the monastery with him the next morning.

Once I had seen him to the walls of Kildare, I returned to my grandmother's hut. Cathbad's driver was already packing the chariot for their journey back to Cruachu.

I entered and found Cathbad and my grandmother sitting on the bench by the fire, eating porridge.

"Deirdre, join us," Grandmother said.

"Thank you. Cathbad, it's good to see you again," I said. "I'm sorry we didn't have time to talk yesterday. I see you're preparing to leave. I don't want to delay you."

"Nonsense, my child. I'm always glad to make time to visit with you. Even more so as the matters pressing us are urgent."

Grandmother got up.

"I'll leave you two to talk. I want to get some strawberries from my garden to send with you, Cathbad. I also gave your man some of my pudding to take back home."

"Ah, thank you, Aoife. I should have married you years ago when I had the chance."

"Indeed you should have."

They both laughed as Grandmother got her basket and went out the door. Cathbad had been happily married for many years, but his beloved wife had died just over a year earlier. She had suffered horribly in the final weeks of her life. Father Ailbe had traveled all the way to Cruachu to treat her, but he said it was a type of illness that had no cure and little way to alleviate the suffering.

"Cathbad, I know you and my grandmother must have discussed the murders of the nuns and the dangers we all face. She'll share with me all the details of your conversation so you don't need to repeat them to me now. But is there anything I should know that might help me find this killer?"

"Yes, my child, the two of us sat up most of the night talking about the situation. We agreed that it must be one of the renegade druids from Finian's group who has taken up his unholy task. I would begin there. Find these associates of Finian and run them to ground. You proceed not only with the king's authority but with my own. Do whatever you need to do with my blessing. I have already sent word to all the druidic leaders of Leinster to aid you in your work. We must stop this man, Deirdre, and stop him quickly. I may have applied a balm to the tempers at the feasting hall last night, but it will not last. The clans of your tribe are ready to go to war, druid against Christian. You occupy a unique position between these factions. You must extinguish this fire before it consumes your people and spreads throughout this island."

"I will do everything in my power," I said. "The nuns should be safe within the walls of the monastery since the king's guards surround them, but they can't live like prisoners forever. They can't carry out their mission of service to others in a fortress. I've got to end this."

"My child, my prayers go with you."

I refilled his bowl with warm porridge and sat back down beside him.

"Cathbad, would you mind if I asked you about something else?"

"Please do, my child."

"Do you think Christianity and the ways of the druids can live together? I suppose I'm asking if you think our church will survive in Ireland—or even if it should. Do you think the teachings of the Gospel are a threat to our traditions?"

He took a large spoonful of porridge and blew on it to cool it.

"Deirdre, did you know that Brigid was a friend of mine from long before you were born? I helped her overcome the opposition among the nobles of your tribe so she could establish her monastery at Kildare. She was truly a holy person, even though she was a Christian. I think those who carry out her work are indeed blessed. If our ancient traditions aren't compatible with her mission of kindness and charity, then it is our ways that are at fault, not hers."

"Cathbad, I wish all druids felt that way. You've always been a most generous man when it comes to the Christians on this island."

"And why wouldn't I be? We druids should always be open to new ideas. We don't think truth can be confined to one narrow form of belief. I have listened carefully to the words of your priests and learned much from the stories of your holy book. I particularly like the parables Jesus told. He seemed to have a keen understanding of human nature and a healthy skepticism regarding dogma. I too wish all of your fellow believers shared his views."

"Most of us do try. I know there are some Christians who see the Gospel as a sword, but we sisters at Kildare prefer to look at it as a cup of living water."

"A pleasing metaphor, my child, which I believe you have borrowed from a story of Jesus sitting by a well. If I remember correctly, he spoke those words to a woman."

"Yes, a Samaritan woman, an outcast of the world in which he lived. Like him, we try to minister to those most in need."

"A noble mission indeed. If all the Christians of Ireland were like the sisters of Brigid, I would sleep better at night."

"What do you mean?"

He reached into his cloak and removed a piece of parchment with a message written in Latin and handed it to me. It was from the abbot of Armagh, demanding that Cathbad allow the establishment of a church at Cruachu to preach the way of salvation to the lost souls of Connacht. He threatened the fires of hell on anyone who stood in his way.

"You can see, my child, that not all Christians share your views. I fear the priests at Armagh have forgotten the ways of the church that Patrick founded there. He was another good man of your faith. I very much enjoyed my discussions with him when I was younger. He traveled freely throughout Ireland

and preached about his god to anyone who would listen, including many druids, though he had only modest success."

"Cathbad, I apologize for the attitude of the abbot of Armagh. Our faith is not about condemnation and damnation. We want only to share the love of God with the people of Ireland."

"I know the abbot is not representative of your faith, at least the faith that Patrick and Brigid preached, but I think your view of Christianity is incomplete."

"In what way?"

"Your religion is not just about love and forgiveness. Jesus gathered the children around him and healed the sick, but he also drove sinners from the Jewish temple with a whip and said that anyone who loved his own family more than him could not be his follower. He himself may not have often spoken of this fiery hell that the abbot mentions in his letter, but his followers certainly do. Your holy book is full of bloodshed, all in the name of your god."

"But Christianity is not about violence."

"Yes, I know you would say it is about love; but would a single, all-powerful god who loves each of us permit so much suffering in this life? Forgive me, Deirdre, but would he have allowed your son to be killed so senselessly? Would he have let my wife die in agony?"

He clenched his fist as he spoke.

"And yet, in spite of all the arguments against Christianity, I know something that no one else in the Order seems to realize."

"What is that?" I asked.

"That in the end, your religion will win."

"You mean you think Christianity will survive in Ireland?"

"I mean much more than that. Your god will someday conquer this island. I see a day when our land is covered with churches and the ways of the druids are forgotten."

"But if you think our religion is unreasonable, how can you suppose it will win?"

"Because when it comes to matters of religion, reason doesn't matter. People crave the assurance that their lives have meaning, and they yearn to live happily after death. What can we druids offer them except a sense of wonder? We tell them that life is often unfair and that the gods aren't always interested in them. We tell them they will indeed be reborn, but only again into this world of pain. But you Christians offer the much simpler view of a god who always loves them, who cares about their least concern, who promises them an eternal life of joy rather than an endless cycle of rebirth. Who wouldn't prefer such a vision to what we druids teach? Yes, you will win. It will take time, but you will win."

I could hear the wind beginning to blow outside.

"I don't want Christianity to replace the old ways, Cathbad. There is so much good, so much truth in what the druids teach. Isn't there another path, one in which we respect and learn from each other?"

"I'm afraid that's wishful thinking, my child, and not even consistent with the doctrines of your own faith. Didn't your Jesus say that he alone was the way, the truth, and the life, so that no one could come to your god except through him? I wish there was another road that lay ahead of us, but I have looked into the future and seen that there is not. The way of the druids—my way and your grandmother's—will fade from Ireland like the light of the setting sun."

He rose from his bench. I walked with him outside, where Grandmother gave him a basket of strawberries, and then I bowed to him in respect. I knew it was against all protocol, but I hugged him. He was surprised but embraced me in turn, then mounted his chariot and rode away.

Chapter Nineteen

With the authority of both the king and the Order, I went to Kildare that same evening and spoke to the captain of the guard. I told him to send armed men to the three known members of Finian's traditionalist circle and bring them to me immediately at a deserted farm near Kildare. It was a violation of Irish law to arrest someone without proper testimony, but at this point I didn't care. By midnight, the guards had returned with the three frightened druids who had been pulled from their beds. One at a time, I questioned them in a leaky barn with rats crawling on the rafters above our heads. The blazing fire, iron chains hanging from the walls, and the two hulking guards who stood next to the men with clubs added a useful touch of intimidation to the proceedings.

They were not an impressive group. All three denied any knowledge of the murders and begged me not to send them to the king to be burned at the stake. I ordered the guards to begin heating an iron rod in the fire. Two of the prisoners were so terrified, they lost control of their bowels. I would normally never have put anyone through such an ordeal, but five nuns were dead and my tribe was about to slip into clan war. In the end, it wasn't necessary to physically harm any of them. Whatever my faults might have been, I was a good judge of human nature. These men were not murderers, simply weak souls who had latched on to Finian like sheep following a bellwether. None of them had the courage to kill another human being.

I told the guards to take shifts and keep the men secure in the barn for the time being. Under no circumstances were they to allow them to leave. I walked back to my grandmother's house, exhausted and utterly frustrated as the sun rose. If none of these men had murdered Alma, then who had? The only possibility was a druid from another tribe, though it was almost impossible for a member of the Order from beyond our borders to move through the kingdom without being noticed by someone. Still, when I reached home, I asked Grandmother to send word to all druids in the area to report to me right away any news of visitors.

"Grandmother, is it possible one of the members of the Order in our tribe has secret sympathies with the traditionalists?"

I was sitting on my bed wrapped in a blanket, eating a bowl of porridge.

"I suppose anything is possible, my child, but it's hard to believe. I know every druid among our people, most of them since they were children. Aside from Finian and those three miscreants you locked away, none has ever expressed traditionalist ideas. Most of that lot are in the far north, and there aren't even many there."

"Well, some druid is killing the nuns of Kildare, and I have run out of ideas for finding him. There were no clues at the murder scenes or on the bodies, except the ones Finian and this second killer wanted us to find. And those clues only make it clear that the murderer has been trained as a druid and plans more sacrifices."

"Maybe there is more we can learn from the murders," she said. "What about the mistletoe?"

"That's what troubles me the most. We don't know if Pelagia had any, but how did Finian get Grainne and Saoirse to drink mistletoe before he killed them? And how did this second killer persuade Alma to drain a cup? I know for a fact that Grainne, sweet as she was, despised Finian and would never have sat at a table with him. And Saoirse was terrified of the man. She would never have opened her door for him, let alone share a drink with him."

"As we said before," she said, "the only explanation that makes any sense is that he somehow forced them to drink the cup by threatening them."

"But that seems so unlikely. Was he threatening to kill their families? Pelagia had no kin or even friends on this island, but the others did. I can see how someone would sacrifice their own lives to protect those they love. But they died with such peaceful expressions on their faces. Would they do that if they were under threat?"

"No," she sighed. "None of it makes sense to me either. The only thing I do know is that we're going to have a bloody war on our hands soon unless we find the killer."

"But what can we do, Grandmother?"

"I have an idea, though you're not going to like it."

"What?"

"The *imbas forosnai*."

"Grandmother, no. I won't let you do that."

"You can hardly stop me, young lady, though it would be easier with your help."

"But you've only done it once before, when you were much younger, and you said it almost killed you then. Even if you don't die, seers can become lost performing that ritual and never return to this world."

"It's dangerous, I agree," she said, "but we are running out of options."

"I can't risk losing you, Grandmother. I just can't."

She sat down and put her arm around me.

"I think I can perform the ritual safely. But, my child, even if I were to die or become lost in the Otherworld, you would be all right. You're not a child anymore. I've got to do this for the sake of our tribe, for the Order, and for the nuns at Kildare. If it works, we might find out who the killer is and be able to stop him before he murders someone else."

"Oh, Grandmother, there must be some other way."

"If you can think of one, please tell me."

I shook my head.

"When will you begin?" I asked.

"I'll start the preparations now. Everything should be ready by tonight. Are we agreed?"

I couldn't stand the thought of her performing such a dangerous ritual, but I didn't know what else to do.

"Yes, I'll help you however I can."

"Good. Now, go find me a stray cat."

Father Ailbe once told me that the church had condemned the *imbas forosnai* as an invocation of Satan, but I knew that the Irish had had no concept of a devil before Christianity arrived in Ireland. The ritual may have been blasphemy, but if any of the unseen spirits of this island could help us find the killer, so be it—and I prayed that God would forgive me.

It took hours, but I finally found a wild cat at a nearby farm and lured it to me with a piece of bacon. When it was done eating, it came to me for more, rubbing against my leg. I grabbed it by the neck and with one forceful twist killed it instantly. I felt terrible doing such a thing, but the needs of the tribe and my friends at the monastery demanded it.

When I returned home, my grandmother took the cat and told me everything was ready. She took the body outside to the butchering table and cut its flesh into thin strips. She could have used a pig or dog, but she had never liked cats, so I wasn't surprised that she had asked me to find one. She took some of the flesh inside the hut and, with her palms turned downward, began chanting over it. After an hour or so, she placed the meat on a rock behind her door. She had once explained to me the reason for this peculiar practice, but I couldn't remember at the moment. I was too busy praying to Brigid and all the saints that this would work.

She prayed once more with her hands over the meat:

> *Strength of sky, light of sun, brilliance of moon,*
> *burning of fire, speed of lightning, swiftness of wind,*
> *depth of sea, firmness of earth, hardness of rock.*

It was an ancient Irish incantation calling on the hidden powers of the world to help her see beyond her mortal sight. Patrick had taken this prayer and changed it into a beautiful hymn, just as Christians borrowed so much from the old religions of Greece and Rome. I used to think this was cheating, but I see now that the nourishing flow across boundaries of faith is a good thing. God knows, the druids borrowed much from the old ones who came before us.

It was starting to grow dark outside. After more prayers, my grandmother turned her palms slowly upward and walked to her bed. Carefully holding her hands in front of her, she lay down on the straw mattress and placed her palms against her cheeks, then closed her eyes. I took her thick wool blanket and spread it over her as she began to drift off into sleep.

I sat next to her the whole night, dozing in my chair and rising only occasionally to place another log on the fire. I knew that sometimes druids would lie in bed for two or three days until a vision came to them. I also knew that sometimes they would awaken after only a few minutes. I was terribly worried, but encouraged that she remained still until sunrise.

When the first light peeked beneath the front door, Grandmother began to shake. Her breathing became heavy and I could feel her heart racing in her chest. I would have tried to awaken her, but I was afraid I would break the spell and she would be lost forever. Suddenly she screamed. I had never been so frightened.

At last she opened her eyes with a strange look on her face.

"Grandmother, are you all right? Are you here with me?"

She wiped her eyes.

"Of course I am, child. Where else would I be?"

She motioned for me to bring her a cup of water and drank it deliberately as I waited quietly.

"I'm fine, Deirdre, though I don't want to go through that again."

"What did you see?"

"It was a most peculiar dream," she said at last. "I was standing on the edge of a dark river in what seemed to be a vast cavern. Around me were hundreds—perhaps thousands—of people, pale and dead, though they could move and speak. An old man in a boat was coming toward us, and the crowd was crying to him with outstretched hands. As he reached the shore, they surged forward, but he beat them back with his paddle, allowing only a few at a time to climb into his little craft after he had examined them closely.

"I looked again at the shore, and there were five women standing beside the boat. They wore the veils of nuns. The strange man looked at them and motioned to them to board the boat. I recognized one as Grainne and called out to her. She turned and gave me a look of great sadness, then climbed into the boat with the others.

"I looked again and suddenly there were two more nuns standing next to me. I couldn't see their faces. Then a tall figure dressed in black came up behind us, wearing a mask. The face on the mask was beautiful, like the paintings of one of your angels at the church. The dark figure then pierced both of the nuns through the chest with a sword. I screamed and tried to stop him but was unable to move. It was as if my feet were fixed to the ground. The two women didn't call out or collapse; they just walked to the boat, climbed in, and sailed away.

"I turned to the person in black and tried to tear the mask away. At last I got my fingers underneath the edge and ripped it off. I had never seen such a face as lay beneath. I can't even begin to describe it. I can only say that it was a monster. That was when I woke up."

She finished the cup of water.

"Grandmother, didn't you recognize any features beneath the mask?"

"No, my child. I'm sorry. I'm afraid the ritual has failed. All I can say is that the nuns of Kildare are still in grave danger."

Chapter Twenty

I had hardly slept in days, but there was no time to waste in bed. After the *imbas forosnai* ritual was over that morning, I left my grandmother's house to go to the monastery. Along the way, I thought about what the images in her dream meant. In spite of the fact that Grandmother had never heard the story from Greek mythology, the man in the boat was obviously Charon, transporting dead souls across the river of death. The five nuns who boarded the boat first were those who had already been killed. The two who were stabbed by the dark figure were the victims yet to come. Did that mean that their fate was already sealed, or could I stop the murders from happening? And who was the dark man? My grandmother said he was tall, but I knew that images in dreams were often symbols not to be taken literally. Most perplexing was the fact that he wore a beautiful mask, but underneath was the face of a monster. Did that mean he was physically handsome, or something else entirely? I needed to talk with Cáma, the interpreter of dreams. I would have to find the time to see her as soon as possible.

The king's guards were at the front gate of the monastery and bowed as they let me through. I hadn't been inside Kildare since I had been expelled, but I felt I needed to report to Sister Anna what was happening, though I wasn't sure that she would even see me. It was still early in the morning, and the yard was empty with only a few cattle moving about in the pen at the far side of the barn. I went to the hut of the abbess and knocked on the door. I knew she would be awake.

"Come in."

She was sitting behind her desk as usual. I could see that she was adding figures on an abacus. She looked up and didn't seem surprised to see me, though she didn't look pleased either. I prepared myself to be yelled at and thrown out of the hut, but she motioned for me to sit in the chair facing her.

"Sister Anna, thank you for seeing me. I know that I'm no longer welcome here, but, as you know, the king has placed me in charge of finding the killer and I thought I should let you know what I have done."

"Proceed," she said.

I told her about the three druids I had questioned and detained in the barn under guard. I told her about my discussion of suspects with my grandmother. I even told her about the *imbas forosnai* and what my grandmother had seen. She was silent when I finished. After a few moments, I got up to leave.

"Thank you for listening, Sister Anna. If you'll excuse me now, I should continue my work."

"One moment," she said. She set the abacus aside and folded her hands together on the desk.

"Yes, Sister Anna?"

"I would like for you to thank your grandmother for me. I do not approve of the *imbas forosnai* ritual, but I know she put herself at great risk to perform it. I only wish it had been successful."

"Thank you, Sister Anna. Is there anything else you would like me to tell her?"

She hesitated for a moment before speaking.

"No. You are dismissed."

I bowed and left her hut to walk back to the gate. I wanted to see Dari and Father Ailbe, but thought it best to leave the monastery before the monks and nuns were up for morning prayers. I was almost at the gate when I heard someone call my name.

"Deirdre, wait!"

It was my cousin Riona. She came running up to me from the barn with a frightened look on her face.

"What's wrong, Riona?"

"I need to talk with you, Deirdre. Can we step outside the gate?"

The guards were reluctant to let her leave the monastery compound, but I told them she wouldn't go far and would be with me the whole time. We went outside the walls to a spreading elm tree and stood beneath the branches.

"What is it, Riona? Are you all right?"

"Yes. No. I mean, I'm not sure."

"Did someone hurt you? What's wrong?"

"I'm fine, but I think I saw something I should tell you about."

"What is it?"

"I couldn't sleep well last night," she said. "I haven't since I got here. I'm grateful to the king's guards for keeping us safe, but I feel trapped in here. I'm used to being on my own with lots of room. I'm also worried about my sheep. Anyway, I got up at maybe three in the morning to take a walk around the yard. The moon was just rising in the east. I walked over to the cattle pens, then went to the shed near the back gate and climbed the ladder so I could look out over the walls. I guess I just wanted to see something beside the inside of this monastery. It was a lovely evening and I could hear sheep bleating in the distance—my own, I think."

"Go on, Riona."

"Well, maybe it was just my imagination, but I saw someone moving away from the monastery. It was too dark to see clearly, but it looked like a tall figure at the edge of the woods to the west, beyond the graveyard. I thought maybe it was one of the guards on patrol, but they always go out in pairs."

"What did this figure look like?"

"He was tall and seemed to be wearing some kind of a dark cloak. I couldn't see a face since he was walking away from me, but just before it reached the woods, he turned to look back. I'm not sure, but he seemed to be a man with a long white beard. I swear he saw me standing there and smiled. I know this sounds crazy, but for a moment I had the feeling it was my grandfather."

"What did you do then?"

"I thought about alerting the guards, but I looked again and the figure was gone. I thought I must have imagined the whole thing. The guards are grumpy enough about having to spend their days watching a bunch of women, I didn't want to wake them to chase after a phantom."

"Take me to the place where you saw this man," I said.

We walked to the west side of the monastery near the edge of the woods. There were tracks on the ground, but the path was often used and there were too many to distinguish the prints of any one person. We searched around the area, but we found nothing.

"I'm sorry to have bothered you, Deirdre," she sighed. "I must have imagined the whole thing. I'm going to lose my mind if I don't get out of this monastery soon."

"It's all right, Riona. We're all on edge lately. Maybe you did see someone. Sometimes hunters are out in the woods at night."

"I doubt it. The moon wasn't bright enough for hunting. I feel so stupid. Let's forget the whole thing. I need to get to morning prayers."

We started to walk back up the path to the monastery. I could hear the noise of doors closing as people left the sleeping quarters to make their way to the church. Riona and I reached the gate.

"Deirdre, do you want to come to prayers with us?"

"I wish I could, but I don't think it's a good idea. I've already seen Sister Anna this morning and it would be pushing my luck to show up at the church. I don't think some of the sisters would be happy to see me anyway."

Riona smiled.

"Such as Eithne? That woman hates me too, probably because I'm your cousin—but I don't care. I'm thinking of loosening the straps on her bed so that they come undone when she lies down tonight."

"Don't pick a fight with her, Riona. She isn't worth the trouble."

"You're probably right. Well, good luck with your search, Deirdre. Please let me know if there's anything I can do to help. And would you go check on my sheep?"

I said I would and kissed her on the cheek, then turned to walk away. Suddenly there was a piercing scream inside the monastery yard. I recognized it as Dari's voice. I rushed inside the gate and saw people running to the church.

Riona and I hurried to the open door. A crowd had gathered, blocking the entrance, but I pushed them away to get inside. Dari was standing in the center aisle, next to the low partition separating the sections for the monks and nuns. She was staring at the front of the church in horror.

There, nailed by her hands to a wooden beam on the front wall of the church and tied with ropes a dozen feet in the air, was the body of Sister Coleen, her throat cut and her arms outstretched as if nailed to a cross.

Chapter Twenty-One

How did he get inside the monastery? How?" demanded Sister Anna.

She was facing the captain of the guard inside the church. We had lowered the body of Sister Coleen from the rafters and taken it to the infirmary. Several of the brothers and sisters were trying to clean up the blood.

The captain was an experienced warrior and a giant of a man named Brogan, who stood about two feet taller than the abbess, but he looked very small at that moment.

"I don't know, Sister Anna," he sputtered. "My men were everywhere guarding the walls and gates. I had two patrols out all night in the surrounding woods. I don't see how anyone could have gotten through."

"Well, someone did and now another of my nuns is dead," she said. "Maybe I should tell the king to send some of his serving girls to replace you, because I'm beginning to think they would have done a better job."

"I'll send a messenger to the king at once and get more men," he said, hanging his head as he spoke. "I'll send out fresh patrols into the woods to track this man down. He won't get away, I promise."

"Spare me your promises, Brogan. Get out and do your job."

The abbess turned and motioned for me to follow her. We left the church and went together to the infirmary. Father Ailbe was bent over the table, examining the body of Sister Coleen.

"Is it the same as with the others, Father?" she asked.

"Yes, Sister Anna. Her stomach contents reveal that Coleen consumed mistletoe before she was killed. Her throat was cut deeply with a single stroke of a very sharp knife while she was unconscious. The lack of bruising on her arms where the ropes held her indicate that she was hauled up after she was already dead."

Sister Anna walked over to the wall near the foot of the table and pounded her hand repeatedly on the post supporting the roof. Tears were running down her cheeks. I had never seen her lose control before, and I didn't know if I should comfort her or leave the room. In the end, I did nothing.

It was only a minute later that she wiped away her tears and turned to me with a face of stone.

"Deirdre, does this fit the order of sacrifices carved onto the body of Sister Saoirse?"

"Yes, Sister Anna."

"I suppose," she said, "the murderer was mocking us by killing his latest victim in our church."

"I suppose so, Sister Anna," I said.

"Six murdered women and seven sacrifices," Father Ailbe said. "One more death yet to come."

"Yes, Abba."

"I don't think this monastery can survive another death," the abbess said. "How on earth could the killer have gotten in? I was in the church at midnight, praying, and at sunrise Sister Coleen is found there, dead. I saw the guards posted at the gates and walking the perimeter of the walls last night and this morning. In spite of what I said in anger to Brogan, the king's men are vigilant and capable. And how in heaven's name did the killer get her to drink mistletoe?"

"Sister Anna," I said, "Riona thinks she saw something strange last night."

"What did she see?"

"She couldn't sleep well last night, so about three in the morning she was by the back gate, standing on the ladder looking out over the walls. She said she may have seen a figure near the woods who looked like he was dressed in black, walking away from the monastery. It was dark, but she said she thought he had a long white beard. She knows it's impossible, but she wonders if it could have been her grandfather."

"The druid sacrificer?" the abbess asked.

"Yes. Did you know him?"

"I knew him. Why didn't she tell the guards? Why didn't she come to me immediately?"

"Because she wasn't sure she had seen anything real."

The abbess stood still for a moment, then grabbed me by the robe and pulled me roughly to Sister Coleen's body.

"Does this look real to you, Deirdre? Does the gaping hole across her throat look real?"

I didn't know what to say.

"Come with me."

I followed the abbess out of the infirmary and across the yard to the back gate. When they had first arrived, the king's men had nailed it shut from the inside with a sturdy oak plank so there would be only one point of entry to the monastery. Sister Anna bent to examine the gate closely. She then struck the plank lightly with her palm. It fell to the ground with a thud.

"Look at these," she said, pointing to the dirt beneath us.

I bent down and picked up six nails. The two still in the wood had been only loosely fixed there. Someone had carefully pushed the nails inward, then somehow lowered the plank to the ground silently and opened the back passage into the monastery. When he left, he had fixed the board so that two nails were barely holding it in place.

"That's how he got in," I said.

"Thank you, Deirdre," the abbess said. "A brilliant observation. I'm so glad the king put you in charge of this investigation. I'll certainly sleep better tonight knowing you're on the job."

"Sister Anna, I—"

"Go, find this phantom. Tell the captain what Sister Riona thinks she saw. I don't care if it's unlikely. And tell your druid friends to keep their eyes open for a tall and very evil man. You might also tell them to lock their doors. Sister Coleen was from the same eastern clan as Sister Saoirse. They are going to be out for blood after this."

The abbess left and returned to her office. I found Brogan and told him about the gate and what Riona thought she had seen. He sent men right away to secure the gate with locks and chains.

I started out the front gate to go to my grandmother's house to ask her to help spread the news to all the druids of the region. Eithne was there waiting for me.

"Six," she said, holding up all the fingers of her right hand and one on her left. "Six nuns. They were my friends, Deirdre."

"They were my friends too, Eithne. I don't have time for this now."

I tried to step around her, but she moved in front of me and shoved me back.

"Eithne," I said, trying to control my temper. "You don't want to start with me."

"Oh, really? I'm so sorry, Deirdre. Are you busy running off to save us? You seem to be doing a miserable job so far. Or maybe you aren't really trying at all. I find it a remarkable coincidence that it's the druids who have been killing these nuns—members of the Order just like you. Could it be that you're protecting one of your own?"

I punched her hard in the jaw. She stumbled but didn't fall, then blocked my next punch and hit me in the face. This fight had been building for a long time, and it felt good to have an outlet for all the pain I was feeling. I ran at her and threw her on the ground, but she hit me in the stomach with her knee. I was the daughter of a warrior and she a peasant girl, but she didn't back down an inch.

I was ready to rip her ears off when suddenly I felt someone grabbing the collar of my tunic from behind. It was Kevin, who in an instant had taken Eithne in the same way and was carrying us both to the nearby water trough. He plunged our heads under and held us there, then pulled us up and did it again. I could barely breathe when he tossed us both on the ground and stood between us.

"Enough!" he shouted.

In all the years I had known him, I had never seen Kevin angry before. The expression on his face brought me to my senses as much as the water.

"We have a madman murdering nuns, and now you two have decided to lend him a hand. I don't care about your stupid childhood rivalries. Stop this, or I swear by holy Jesus himself I will beat some sense into both of you. Do you understand me?"

We mumbled our agreement and got up off the ground. While Eithne went back to the nuns' quarters to wash up, I wiped the blood from my face and started out of the gate. Across the yard, I could see Sister Anna standing outside her office. She shook her head and went back inside.

Chapter Twenty-Two

J ust off the path to Grandmother's house, beneath a grove
of trees, was a clearing with a spring-fed well of clear,
cold water. I didn't want to show up at her door with my
face covered in dried blood, so I walked down the side trail to
wash myself.

I had come here many times in my life when I was troubled. It
was a favorite place of mine, and was sacred to women from ages
long forgotten. There was a crumbling stone altar to an unknown
goddess next to the spring and a more recent cross dedicated to
our founder Brigid. I was pleased to see that someone had been
here recently and placed a wreath of bright spring flowers on
the altar and another on the cross. The well wasn't often visited
anymore, and it pained me to see it in neglect.

I took off my robe and knelt by the water, splashing it on my face and scrubbing the dried blood from my mouth. I felt so foolish for having a fight with Eithne in the middle of all that was going on. Kevin was right. There was no time for petty conflicts when a murderer was on the loose.

Kneeling there before the altar and cross, I closed my eyes and prayed:

"Holy saint or goddess, whoever you might be, please help me find the man who is killing my friends. I'm running out of time."

"Time is always the problem, isn't it?"

I jumped up so fast at the sound of the voice that I slipped and fell back down on the grass. An old woman was standing behind me.

"I'm so sorry, my dear," she said. "I didn't mean to frighten you. I was coming to visit the well and saw you here. I wasn't trying to eavesdrop. Do you mind if I sit with you for a moment? My old bones could use a rest."

I remembered my manners at last.

"Of course. Please have a seat."

She sat down on a flat stone beside me. I could see that she was very old, more ancient than Father Ailbe. Yet for a moment when the reflection of the sun on the water struck her face, she looked young and beautiful. I rubbed my eyes and she was old again. It must have been a trick of the light.

"I'm glad to have some company," she said. "Not many people come here any more like they did in the old days. Are you on a long journey?"

"No, I'm just on the way to my grandmother's house down the road. I'm coming from the monastery at Kildare where I am—or at least I was—a nun."

"Ah, a sister of the holy fire. I remember Brigid well. She always cared for those poor souls who had nowhere else to turn. A woman like that is truly blessed."

"You knew Brigid? Are you a Christian, grandmother?"

She smiled as she shook her head.

"No, my child. I have great respect for your god, but I'm afraid I can't follow him. Personally I don't think he should have let himself be nailed to that tree, though I have to admire his courage."

She reached into her small satchel and pulled out a ripe red apple.

"Would you like one, my dear? I've been gathering them."

My eyes grew wide.

"How can you have fresh apples? They're out of season."

"Well, you just have to know where to look."

I took the apple and bit into it. I had never tasted anything so sweet in my life.

"If you don't mind my saying so, my child," the old woman said, "you look like someone with the cares of the world on her shoulders."

I normally didn't share my problems with strangers, but there was something about this woman that drew me out.

"Yes, I don't think I've ever felt so burdened in my life. I'm sure you've heard about the murders of the sisters of Brigid at the monastery. They were wonderful women and they were killed in the most horrible ways. The king has put me in charge of finding the murderers. I thought there was just one and I had caught him, but now there's another. To make matters worse, my tribe is on the brink of war and my life is falling apart. I became a nun after my son died because I thought it might bring me peace. He was only a year old, so beautiful and full of life. I tried to save him, but I couldn't. I seem to be a failure as a nun and a druid and a mother. I sometimes think the world would be better off if I had never been born."

I wiped my eyes on my cloak as the old woman sat silently. She stared at the water for a long time before she spoke.

"My child, I wish I could make all the pain go away. If more years of experience than you can imagine are worth anything, then I will tell you that life is indeed worth living. I'm sure you've done far more good than you know, touched many people during your years on this earth, and will touch many more in the time ahead of you. I know you have suffered greatly. There can be no greater pain for a woman than to watch a life she brought into the world pass away. No mother or father or husband can reach so deeply into a woman's soul. I have borne many children myself and lost most of them as time has passed. You never forget them, never love them less. All I can say is that life does go on and there can be happiness, even joy, mixed with the sorrow of memory."

I was weeping openly now. The old woman moved closer to me and put her arm around me as we sat side by side. She held me until at last the tears began to ease.

"As for the rest, what has happened to the sisters of Brigid is terrible. For someone to think they bring about good by such sacrifices is blasphemy to all that is holy. But in the end, Deirdre, balance will be restored."

I wiped my eyes again and stared at her.

"How can you know who I am? Are you a druid? Do you have the gift of sight? By what name may I call you?"

She laughed gently and shook her head.

"No, my dear, I would make a poor druid and I'm afraid my sight has faded over the years. Sometimes I can't even remember my own name. Let's just say that I have lived a long time. I've traveled up and down this island for ages and talked with countless people. I've even been to other lands from time to time and seen towering mountains, endless deserts, and turquoise seas filled with beautiful creatures, though it's the people I remember most.

"But wherever I go, I always come back to this spring. I suppose it feels like home. Pilgrims used to come here from all over this island in the days when the Romans ruled across the sea. But this place was sacred long before then. Before there was sowing and harvesting, when giant red deer roamed these forests, the women of this land used to come here on holy days and sing lovely songs to the spirits of the earth, raising their voices to the sky. It's so sad to think this spring is in ruin now, fallen like so much in the world."

"How could you know all this?"

She smiled.

"Oh, they're just stories from a foolish old woman. Pay them no mind, my dear."

I started to ask her more, but the smell of smoke suddenly drifted over the spring. She looked at me with sadness and great compassion.

"I'm afraid you must be on your way, my child."

The smell of smoke was growing stronger and I heard the sound of voices shouting in the distance from the direction of my grandmother's home. I got up in a panic and began to hurry down the path. At the edge of the clearing, I turned back for a moment, but the old woman was gone.

By the time I got to Grandmother's clearing, her house was engulfed in flames. I called out for her frantically and tried to go inside, but the heat was so great that it drove me back. I kept calling to her and running around the house until finally I saw a figure lying in the grass by the barn.

It was my grandmother. There was blood all over her face and tunic, but she was alive.

"No! Dear God, no! Grandmother, what happened? Who did this?" I asked frantically as I wiped the blood away.

She wasn't able to speak at first, but at last she whispered a single word.

"Christians."

Chapter Twenty-Three

Her arm is broken and she has a concussion. The bruises on her face will heal, but the stab wound is deep, piercing her spleen. I'm sorry, Deirdre, but I'm not sure she will live."

I was in the monastery infirmary late that same morning with Father Ailbe, Dari, and Sister Anna. I had carried Grandmother in my arms back to Kildare. Now she was lying unconscious on one of the beds, with bandages on her head and abdomen. She had a splint fixed on her arm, and her left eye was swollen shut.

Even though I had seen such horrors over the last few weeks, nothing had prepared me for this. I couldn't believe this was really happening. Surely any moment my grandmother would wake up and insist we were all making a fuss over nothing, then she would jump out of bed and hurry back to her hut. But she didn't move. The woman who had raised me, loved me, and taught me so much about life was dying, attacked by my fellow Christians. None of this made any sense. My head was spinning and I felt like I was about to faint.

"Is there anything more you can do, Abba?"

"Not at the moment, my child. I've performed surgery and stopped the internal bleeding, but she has lost a lot of blood. If you hadn't been there right away to bring her here, she would be dead. The only thing we can do now is wait and pray."

"I'm so sorry, Deirdre," Sister Anna said. "I've had my differences with your grandmother, but she is a fine woman. Whoever did this is no true Christian."

"It must have been a gang of thugs from the eastern clans," I said. "They attacked a druid because of the murders of their kinswomen. My grandmother was an easy target."

"Is there anything left of her home?" Dari asked.

"No. It's just a charred ruin now. They even killed her cow."

Sister Anna knelt by Grandmother's bed and prayed, then kissed her on the cheek and stood up.

"The western clans will have already heard about your grandmother," said Sister Anna. "She is highly respected among them. They won't let this go unanswered."

"Saoirse's Christian clan is just over the plain to the east of the monastery," I said.

"I imagine it was some of their young men who did this to your grandmother," the abbess said. "They're probably preparing for battle now."

"As we said before, a battle between two clans will quickly lead to full tribal war," Father Ailbe said.

"Yes," the abbess replied, "and Kildare sits in the middle of the plain between east and west. If it comes to war, it will happen here. We must prepare ourselves."

"Are we going to fight for the eastern clans?" Dari asked.

"Of course not," Sister Anna said. "But we are going to defend ourselves. The king will withdraw his men from here to fight if war comes. We must be ready to hold these walls on our own. Dari, go tell the sisters and brothers to arm themselves. I don't want us to kill anyone, but I will not let this monastery be destroyed."

Dari and Sister Anna left. I sat down next to Grandmother's bed with Father Ailbe and held her hand. She looked so frail. I had lost my father before I was born and my mother when I was a young child. My grandmother had raised me and was the only family I had ever known. The thought of losing her was terrifying.

"Deirdre, there's nothing more you can do for her," Father Ailbe said. "I promise I'll take good care of her and send word if anything changes."

"How can I leave her, Abba?"

"I know it's hard, but your grandmother would be the first to say that you have important work to do. Many people are going to die if war comes—and you may be the only one who can stop it."

I nodded and wiped my eyes.

"I should go to the western clans and try to talk them out of retaliating, if it isn't already too late. They might listen to me. What do you think is going to happen?"

He sighed deeply.

"My child, I wish I knew. It's like the story of Pandora's jar. Once evil has escaped into this world, it's very difficult to get it back under control. War and hatred feed on fear and anger, and there's plenty of that on all sides."

"Who do you think will win?"

"No one wins a war, Deirdre. But if I had to guess, I would say the king and the eastern clans will be victorious in the end. However, the cost to the tribe will be so great that we may all end up losing everything."

I kissed him and my grandmother, put my harp in its case, and left my sword in the infirmary. I then hurried from the monastery toward the stronghold of Brion, leader of the western clans.

As I climbed the path and came at last over the highest point on the trail, I saw smoke rising in the valley below me and knew that I was too late. I heard the wailing of women in the distance and started to run. In a large field beyond the forest in the valley, I saw a sight I will never forget. There were perhaps two dozen men lying on the ground, most dead but a few still barely moving. There had been a battle here not more than an hour ago. It must have been one of the eastern clans on their way west to attack one of Brion's outlying farmsteads. But the western men must have gotten word of their plans and been lying in wait for them in the forest.

The dead and dying men were all naked, having been stripped of their weapons, jewelry, and clothing by the victors. A few who must have been the leaders had been decapitated and their heads taken as trophies. Everywhere the ground was stained with blood.

The women who had followed the men on the raid were wives, sisters, and mothers, now mourning the fallen and caring for the wounded. There was no time to feel pity or even think. I quickly ran to help a young man who was still alive. An older woman who must have been his mother was kneeling next to him. He had been stabbed in the chest with a spear and had a large sucking wound. His mouth was full of blood as he struggled to breathe, but there was nothing I could do.

Mercifully, just as I turned to grab some rags out of my satchel, he rolled his head to the side and died with his eyes wide open.

I moved to the next man, who was lying on the ground while a young woman, probably his wife, knelt over him. She was trying to stop the bleeding from a sword that had slashed his right arm just above the elbow all the way through the bone. She had done a good job, but the wound required a new tourniquet that I applied by twisting a strip of cloth tightly with a stick. I had seen wounds like this before and told her I would need to amputate if he were going to live, though I knew he might die in any case. She nodded numbly and began to build a small fire next to him as I instructed her. If Father Ailbe had been there, he could have given the man a sedative herb and used his saw to take the arm off quickly, but all I had was my knife.

When the fire was ready, I staked his injured arm to the ground with a rope, placed the blade in the fire to heat, and told the woman to hold him down tightly no matter what happened. Hoping the man would stay unconscious, I began to cut through his flesh. He awoke immediately and began to scream. Fortunately, the sword had done most of the work for me so that all I had to do was slice through what remained of the tissue holding his arm to his body. He screamed even louder when I took a bundle of burning sticks from the fire and held them underneath the severed stump to cauterize the wound. I told his wife to keep the tourniquet tight, then I moved on to the next man. I tried not to think about the fact that these may have been the same men who had attacked my grandmother.

By late afternoon, the survivors had been loaded onto carts and taken back to the east. There were not enough people to see to the dead, so they were left unburied in the field. Unable to bear the stench of the rotting flesh on a summer's day, I walked about half a mile away and sat beneath a willow tree by a stream. In the distance, I could hear ravens flocking to the feast.

I wanted to cry, scream, or curse God, but it wouldn't do any good. All I could do was sit beneath the tree and try to breathe. I had sung before kings many times about the glory of war, about Irish warriors fighting to the death in heroic combat; I had always loved the stories of Greeks slaying their enemies before the walls of Troy; but I had never seen the aftermath of a real battle with my own eyes—the dead lying in dark red mud, the broken bodies, the shattered lives. There was nothing heroic about any of it.

I knew now that war was inevitable. The eastern clans would not forgive this attack. The king would have to side against the western clans. Word would have reached him already and he would have withdrawn his men from the monastery by now. He would need every warrior he had in the coming fight.

But there was still one nun in danger of being brutally murdered, still one sacrifice to perform. I knew the killer would not stop because there was war. The war would in fact make it easier for him. Who would care about a single nun when so many men would soon be dying?

I knew then that my place was at the monastery. I was no longer a sister of holy Brigid, but I would not leave my friends to face a killer or an army without me.

I ran back over the hills and through the forest to Kildare, my harp at my side. I could see the brothers and sisters on the walls of the monastery as I drew near. The king had indeed withdrawn his men.

As I got to the gate, Sister Garwen came running to me.

"Deirdre, Deirdre! They're gone!"

"Yes, Garwen, I can see the soldiers are gone. Don't worry. We'll be all right. I'm going to stay here. I can fight as well as any man."

"No, no, not the soldiers."

She was so frantic that she could barely speak.

"What are you talking about, then?"

"Riona and Dari. We can't find them anywhere. They're gone."

"What do you mean?" I shouted. "When did you see them last? Are you sure they're not here?"

I was shaking Garwen to get her to calm down and answer me, but it was no use. Kevin and three of the sisters ran out of the gate. Sister Anna and Father Ailbe were close behind.

"They were here for midday meal about six hours ago," Kevin said, "just after you left. Then word arrived from the king, withdrawing all the soldiers. There was so much commotion with all the guards leaving that it was hard to know who was going where. We collected our weapons and were all on the walls an hour later, but Riona and Dari could have left before that without anyone seeing them. We've searched every corner of the monastery. They're not here."

"But how could anyone force them both out of the monastery at the same time in broad daylight?" I demanded.

"We don't know," said Sister Anna. "The back gate is still chained shut. They must have gone out the front. One of the guards as he was leaving said he might have seen two nuns heading into the woods to the west, but he wasn't sure."

"Were they alone?" I asked.

"He didn't know."

"I'm going to find them," I said.

"I'll go with you," said Kevin.

"No," I insisted. "You're needed here. You're the best fighter we have. If anyone attacks Kildare, there are going to be more than just two nuns in danger. I'm going to find this monster myself and kill him before he can hurt Dari or Riona."

I handed my harp to Father Ailbe to watch for me. Then I hugged him quickly, got my sword from the infirmary, and ran down the path to the west.

It was already growing dark, but I found two sets of footprints leading down a side path from the main trail. The footprints were far apart and deep, so I knew both women were running. I was relieved to see that there was not a third person with them, but I couldn't imagine why they would run off by themselves into the forest when there was still a madman on the loose. And why wouldn't they tell anyone where they were going? I had a terrible feeling that they were heading into a trap.

I followed the tracks for several miles through thick forests of elm and ash until I reached a small clearing. It was night now, but the stars were bright in the sky. I could see the comet Sinann had discovered near the constellation of the Great Bear to the north. Its red tail had grown longer and more menacing in the last few days.

On top of a low hill about a mile away I saw the flicker of a fire. I had been on that hill before. It was a druid temple used by the western clans of our tribe for sacrifices on holy days. The sacred places of the Order were not made of stone like those of the Greeks and Romans, but were walled enclosures of interlacing boughs about the height of a man and perhaps a hundred feet across. They were open to the sky and aligned with the rising of the sun on the summer or winter solstice. There were no stone statues inside, but some temples had rough wooden images of gods and goddesses carved on standing logs. There was always an altar for animal sacrifice on the northern side of the enclosures, but most of the interior was open space for the gathering of worshipers. The first travelers from the Mediterranean world who had visited our island centuries ago found these temples unimpressive and concluded that we were a barbarian people without any religious sensibility. They associated serious worship of the gods with elaborate architecture and grand marble images covered in gold. For the Irish, it was just the opposite. True religious devotion was a matter of a simplicity of communion between humans and the divine.

I began to run in long strides up the hill toward the temple. When I grew close to the top, I slowed and took my sword from my belt. The single wooden gate to the temple area was shut and there was no sound coming from inside. I walked silently to the gate and eased up the latch. I pushed the gate open just a few inches and saw a small fire burning near the altar. With my sword ready, I entered the enclosure.

I couldn't see anyone at first, but then at the far end of the temple I saw a large wicker cage surrounded by firewood and a person in the robes of a nun slumped on the ground inside. It was Dari.

At that moment I felt something hard strike me on the head from behind. I staggered and struggled to keep my balance, but then I fell on my back beneath the altar. The last thing I remembered was the stars shining in the sky and a figure in black standing over me. Then everything was darkness.

Chapter Twenty-Four

When I woke up, it was still dark. The first thing I remember feeling was surprise that I was alive.

My head was throbbing and I couldn't move. I was sitting tied to a post next to the wicker cage. Dari was still asleep, unconscious, or dead, I couldn't tell which. She had the same calm look on her face as the other victims. I looked around but couldn't see anyone else. I called out to Dari, but there was no answer.

"She's still alive, Deirdre."

Riona was standing alone by the gate of the temple.

"Riona, quick, untie me so we can get Dari out of here before he comes back! The monastery is preparing for war. No one is coming to help us."

She walked over to me slowly and bent down. She took off her veil and began wiping the blood off my face.

"Never mind that now, Riona. Untie me! Hurry!"

She stood facing me with a look of great sadness.

"I'm sorry, Deirdre, I can't untie you."

"What? Why? He'll be back any minute."

"There's no one else here. There never was."

"What are you talking about? He hit me on the head and tied me up."

"I'm afraid *I* did that."

"What? What are you talking about?"

"I didn't want to. I never planned to hurt you. I thought I would be done before anyone got here."

"Done with what?"

She tied the bloody veil back onto her neck.

"The sacrifice."

She stood facing me, waiting for the words to sink in.

"Riona . . . no. That's not possible."

She looked exhausted, but calm and determined.

"Deirdre, I never meant for you to know. I never meant for anyone to know."

"But *why*? And how could it be you? You're not even a druid."

"I have a little while before Dari's mistletoe wears off, so I guess I can tell you. It would feel good to explain it all to someone."

She sat down on the dirt in front of me.

"I did it for the monastery. For the church. For all the Christians of Ireland."

I tried working on the ropes behind me. They were so tight that they were cutting off my blood supply. But I had to keep her talking. I had to keep Dari alive.

"Christianity is failing on this island, Deirdre. It's been almost a century since Patrick arrived. In all that time, how much impact has the Gospel made? A few dozen churches, a handful of monasteries. The people here still live in darkness, worshiping false gods. The druids still fill their hearts with lies. Oh, I know most of them mean well, people like Aunt Aoife, but the seeds of truth can't take root here while there are so many weeds choking them. The only way for the church to prosper here is for the druids to perish."

I kept working at the ropes. I couldn't move them at all.

"But Riona, why would you kill nuns? Why would you work with Finian?"

She looked puzzled.

"Finian? I never worked with him. Why would you think that?"

"Because he killed the first four sisters."

"Finian didn't kill anyone, Deirdre. It was always me."

This was unreal. I kept expecting to wake up. But I knew this was no dream.

"But Finian died at the stake without saying a word."

"I guess he wanted a martyr's death. Or maybe he knew it would do no good to protest after I gave my testimony to the king."

"Then why, Riona? Why would you kill those women?"

"Like I said, the church is in trouble. The light of Christ is going to die on this island unless something happens to rid us of the druids."

"By killing nuns? Are you insane?"

"No, Deirdre, not insane, just very, very tired. You can't imagine how hard this has been on me. Do you know what it's like to take somebody's life? I wished a thousand times I could have accomplished all this by simply dying myself. I would have gladly sacrificed my own life instead of theirs."

She closed her eyes and sighed deeply.

"But I knew that wouldn't be good enough. I had to do something so shocking, it would turn the people against the

Order. I had to make them think druids were killing the gentle sisters of Kildare. I knew that the Christian clans in the east and their allies would rise against the Order if I could provoke them enough. And now the war is about to begin. It will burn away the druids of Ireland. It won't be easy and it won't happen all at once, but the fire of the Gospel will spread throughout this land."

I felt one of the ropes on my wrist loosening just a bit.

"Riona, how could you know how to do these sacrifices? You're not a druid. No druid in his right mind would ever have told you."

"Ah, that's true, Deirdre. But a druid *not* in his right mind did."

"What do you mean?"

"About two months ago, I was at my farm looking after the sheep one evening when an old druid came wandering up my path. He was mumbling to himself about coming home, coming home. I asked him who he was, but he didn't answer me. I took him inside the house and gave him a cup of water and something to eat. He looked around, asking why everything had been moved. I realized then that he was my grandfather, the man who had cursed my parents so long ago."

"Your grandfather? The druid sacrificer?"

"Yes. I confess I thought about killing him then and there. I could have slit his throat like a sheep and buried him in the woods. No one would have ever known. But I put him in my bed and he fell asleep, still mumbling. He's dead now."

"You killed him? But you said you thought you saw your grandfather in the woods outside the monastery yesterday. The board on the gate was loose."

"The board was easy to loosen from the inside to make it look like someone had entered from the outside. And I said a lot of things to mislead people, Deirdre. I had to. But no, I didn't kill my grandfather. He died about a week later in his sleep. But not before I got what I wanted from him."

"What was that?"

The outer rope on my hands was almost off. If I could just twist my hands enough to loosen the inner one.

"The secrets of druid sacrifices. I came up with the idea that first night. It was as if God had sent the man to me to reveal with his final breath the means to destroy the Order. He was completely demented. I don't know how he had wandered back to the farm after all those years, but I suppose memories of youth are strong. He didn't know who I was or what he was doing, but he knew the details of the seven sacrifices like the back of his hand. All it took was patience as I questioned him. After two days, he had revealed everything to me, even the recipe for the mistletoe drink. When he died, I gave him a decent burial. I am a Christian, after all."

"So Finian never attacked you at your farm?"

"No, of course not. I knew you would be coming by to visit that morning. I staged the whole thing to make Finian look guilty and rouse anger against the druids."

"You almost strangled yourself and killed your own dogs?"

She hesitated for a moment.

"Yes. The choking was easy enough, though it did hurt quite a bit. But my dogs, my beautiful dogs. . . ."

The inner rope was slowly coming loose now.

"But how did you get the nuns to drink the mistletoe?"

"Oh, that was easy. I stopped at each of their hermitages for a visit and offered them some mead from a bottle in my satchel. The mistletoe was mixed into it in the precise amount. I couldn't let them suffer, except for Fedelm, unfortunately, who had to suffer as part of the ritual."

"But how could you kill them? They were fellow sisters of holy Brigid. How could you hate them so much?"

She looked astonished.

"Hate them? Deirdre, I loved them all. I pray for them every day."

She stood up.

"I need to finish before Dari wakes up."

She walked over to the small fire by the altar and got a blazing stick. The woodpile beneath Dari's cage was as dry as a bone. It would be a raging inferno in moments.

"For God's sake, Riona, no! Even if you believe you killed the others for some noble reason, you don't need to hurt Dari. Your war is about to start. You've won. You've accomplished what you set out to do. Please, don't kill her, I beg you."

She knelt down beside me again.

"I have to, Deirdre. Don't you understand? I have to complete the seven sacrifices. It will make the anger against the druids even greater when they find her body. The cycle will be complete. Seven sacrifices, seven victims. Or I suppose I should say eight."

She took a bottle from her satchel and pulled out the stopper.

"Please drink this, Deirdre. I don't want you to suffer either."

"Are you crazy? You think I'm going to drink that so you can kill me?"

"I'm going to kill you anyway, Deirdre. I can't let you live to tell people who the real killer is. That would ruin everything."

She grabbed my head and tried to force the drink into my mouth, but I turned away and fought her off.

"Deirdre, I am trying to help you. I don't want you to feel pain. I don't want you to have to watch Dari die. Please drink it."

I pursed my lips together tightly. Riona sighed and gave up.

"It's your choice. I'm so sorry, Deirdre."

She began walking toward Dari's pyre with the burning stick.

"Wait, Riona! Take me instead. I'll drink the mistletoe, then put me in the cage instead of her. She doesn't have to die."

"I'm sorry, Deirdre. I wish that would work, but it's too late. I told Dari you had sent a message saying that it was a matter of life or death for the two of us to meet you here and that we were to tell no one. I knew none of the other nuns would dare leave the monastery, but Dari would if she thought you were in danger. If I let her go, she would know I lied and tell everyone. I can't let her live."

She tossed the burning brand onto the dry kindling beneath Dari.

"NO!"

"I'm sorry, Deirdre. I'm so sorry."

The fire was raging in a matter of seconds. It was almost to the bottom of the cage.

It was then that I broke through the last rope.

I jumped up and hurled myself at Riona in one desperate motion. I knocked her down hard so that she fell forward into the fire. I then ran to the cage and tore open the door, pulling Dari out just as her robes were starting to burn. I quickly put them out and dragged her to the wall at the edge of the temple. I turned to save Riona, but it was too late. She was trapped deep in the fire, writhing and screaming as she was devoured by the flames.

Chapter Twenty-Five

D ari was groggy as we left the druid temple, but there was no time to waste. I wrapped her arm around my shoulder and half-dragged her down the path and back through the woods on the trail to Kildare.

It would be dawn soon, and I knew the armies of the eastern and western clans would be gathering near the monastery. My only hope to prevent a slaughter was to somehow convince them of the truth, which I scarcely believed myself. I hoped it would work, but I had serious doubts. Blood had already been spilled on both sides, and Irish warriors were not known for listening to reason.

By the time we got to the edge of the woods near the monastery, it was daylight and Dari was walking mostly on her own.

I explained to her what had happened as quickly as I could. I could see the monks and nuns on the walls in the distance. I could also hear the sounds of shouting and the movement of men in the plain on the far side of Kildare.

I led Dari to the gate of the monastery, where Father Ailbe and Sister Anna met us.

"Deirdre, what happened? Where is Riona?" demanded the abbess.

"She's dead. I'm sorry, but I don't have time to explain now. I've got to try to stop this battle."

Father Ailbe took Dari from me and helped steady her.

"Abba, is my grandmother still alive?"

"Yes, though I'm afraid I'm still not sure if she will live."

He handed me my harp.

"I think you might need this," he said.

"Thank you, Abba."

"Is there anything you need from me?" Sister Anna asked.

"Your prayers, please. I don't see how this is going to work."

I ran along the walls to the far side of the monastery and looked down the hill to the wide plain below.

There were two armies before me. The eastern clans with King Dúnlaing at their head numbered perhaps five hundred men. The lines of the western clans led by Brion were only slightly smaller. The warriors of both sides were magnificent to see. Most were dressed in woolen pants and bright red tunics that would hide the blood from any wounds. Over the tunics were finely worked shirts of black chain mail. Each man had a razor-sharp sword on a belt around his waist and a long-headed spear in his right hand. Their tall shields were made of wood and painted with intricate and colorful designs unique to each clan. Each warrior wore a helmet of polished bronze on his head with loose earpieces that hung down, protecting the sides of his head, and were tied with a leather thong under the chin.

As I drew closer, I could see that the king and the clan leaders were standing in wooden chariots with their drivers kneeling in front of them. Like most Irish horses, the two animals pulling each chariot were small but thick in the chest for endurance. Chariots were mostly for show and would not be used to charge the lines. The leaders would dismount from them to fight while their drivers waited nearby. There were a few cavalrymen on horses moving around the edges of the lines, but Leinstermen traditionally favored fighting on foot. I saw that a few of the more zealous warriors in the front of both lines had stripped off all their armor and clothing in the old manner to show their contempt for death and were shouting insults across the field to the other side.

With my bardic robe draped around my shoulders and my harp in my hands, I marched alone down the hill into the space between the two armies. No one would dare to stop a bard. All the sisters and brothers were watching me from the nearby walls.

I struck the strings of the harp and began to play a somber tune as loudly as I could. When both sides had quieted, I began to sing:

> The stories of old speak of men waging war.
> Brave men, great men, men of honor.
> They feared nothing and bowed to no one.
> But they all heard the words of a bard.

"Listen to me, all of you!" I shouted. "I demand that the leaders of each army come to me here with their captains."

The king and Brion both looked surprised that a small woman with a harp was giving them orders just as they were preparing to fight. Neither side moved.

"If you do not obey me, I will compose a satire on you all. You and your sons for seven generations will bear the shame of defying me!"

The leaders looked at the men beside them and at last signaled their charioteers to move forward to the center of the plain. When they came near and stopped, I spoke in a voice both armies could hear. In bardic school I had been trained to make my voice carry when needed. I knew I had to hold their attention and speak quickly. This was not a time for nuance.

"There is no honor in what you do here today. You fight for a lie!"

There were some angry shouts from both lines, but I spoke louder still.

"You think the druids have murdered the sisters of Kildare, but in fact it was one of their own nuns who killed them."

There was a gasp from all sides and shouts of disbelief. "Hear me! She wanted to turn all of you against each other. And you have fallen into her trap like rabbits, caught in the snares of a woman."

I had always found that the best way to stop men from doing something stupid was to play on their pride.

"I will explain everything to your leaders, but believe me when I proclaim on my honor as a bard that the druids had nothing to do with these murders."

"Even if that's true," shouted Saoirse's father from his chariot, "blood has been spilled. My warriors were ambushed and killed by the cowards of the western clans. Their spirits cry out for vengeance!"

A shout arose from the men behind him.

"We curse the spirits of your men," shouted Brion from the opposite side. "They attacked a great druid—your own grandmother, Deirdre. You speak of cowards, but these men have no honor."

Now a shout arose from the ranks of the western clans. Spears began to pound against shields on both sides. This wasn't going to work. Tempers had gone too far.

"You want blood?" I shouted, raising my arms for silence. "So be it."

I marched up to King Dúnlaing and spoke to him directly, making sure the whole army could hear me.

"My lord, you are the ruler of this tribe. No man on either side of this field doubts your wisdom and courage. Your eastern warriors demand druid blood, your western clans want Christian blood. I will give you both."

I drew my sword and handed it to the king.

"This is the weapon my father used to defend this tribe against the Uí Néill. He stood beside many of the elder warriors here today, fighting for the lives of eastern and western clans of this tribe alike. He died so that this tribe might prosper as one people—and I will do no less."

I took off my bardic robe and spread it on the ground.

"I am both a druid and a Christian," I shouted. "Let my blood satisfy what you all desire. Let me be the final sacrifice."

I then knelt on my robes at the foot of the king and bowed my head for the blow that would sever it from my body.

There was a silence across the whole plain. I could feel the eyes of a thousand people watching me, including the sisters and brothers at the monastery. I knew Dari would be there on the walls with Father Ailbe and Sister Anna and the rest of the community. I said a final prayer.

Then the king spoke.

"Deirdre, daughter of Sualdam, the blood of your father truly runs in your veins. Rise and stand beside me."

I stood up, shaking, and stood next to the king.

"Hear me, all of you, eastern and western clans alike. I am the king of this tribe and I swear by the gods of this tribe that no blood will be shed today, whether from a bard or a warrior. I pledge to you all my word as king that this ends here, now. There will be no further vengeance by any clan. We cannot weaken ourselves so that outsiders take our land. Divided, we are prey for our enemies. United, we are strong. We are one people and always will be."

Dúnlaing then walked to the chariot of Brion and stood waiting. The leader of the western clans hesitated only for a moment, then dismounted and stood next to the king. Dúnlaing held out his hand, and at last Brion took it.

A shout arose from both sides, building slowly at first, then echoing across the plain. I could hear the voices of the sisters and brothers on the walls join in. It was a roar that must have been heard all the way to the borders of the Uí Néill. These were brave warriors who would have gladly laid down their lives for their clans that day, but they knew that no one would have prospered from this war. The tribe united was the greatest victory of all.

Chapter Twenty-Six

I met with King Dúnlaing and the clan leaders in the monastery church a short while later. Father Ailbe and Sister Anna were there as well. Tempers were still raw and there were many questions, but by the end of the meeting I was able to convince everyone of the truth. The king was the last of the nobles to leave.

"We all owe you a great debt of gratitude, Deirdre."

"My lord, you owe me nothing. It was my honor and duty to serve my king. I only wish I could have found the killer sooner so that there would have been fewer deaths and less grief."

He smiled and took a magnificent golden torque from his neck and placed it on mine. I tried to protest, but he would have none of it. He then left me alone in the church with Father Ailbe and Sister Anna.

"Abba, may I see Grandmother now?"

"Of course."

"Deirdre," said Sister Anna, "when you are done, please come to my office."

I went to the infirmary and found Dari resting on a cot. I hugged her as she sat up in bed. It was only then that I had time to realize how glad I was that she was alive.

"You were amazing, Deirdre. Weren't you scared? Did you really think the king would have cut off your head?"

"I was terrified. And yes, I think the king would have cut off my head to save the tribe. I was ready for him to. I would have done anything to stop the chaos that would have come from the war. Thank God, sometimes being willing to die is just as good as the real thing."

Squeezing Dari's hand one last time, I walked across the room to my grandmother's bed. Her face was even more bruised and swollen than before. She looked as if she were barely hanging on to life. I sat down on her bed and touched her cheek. Her one good eye opened slightly.

"Deirdre?"

"Yes, Grandmother. Don't try to talk. You were badly hurt. You're here at the monastery. Father Ailbe is taking good care of you. You need to rest."

"Rest. Yes."

She drifted off to sleep again.

I walked away from her to talk with Father Ailbe.

"Abba, is there anything more you can do?"

He took my hand in his.

"I'm sorry, my child, but I've done all I can. The bleeding inside has stopped, but she was badly hurt and she's not a young woman anymore. It's now in the hands of God."

He held me as I cried. Dari joined us and hugged me as well. After a few minutes, I pulled myself together.

"I need to go see Sister Anna."

"What do you think she'll say?" Dari asked. "I wonder if she'll let you back in the monastery. I'd think she would have to, after what you did on the battlefield."

"I don't think that has anything to do with being a nun," I said. "Christians are supposed to turn the other cheek, but Sister Anna is not a forgiving person."

I left the infirmary and walked across the monastery yard. Several of the sisters and brothers came up and thanked me. The abbess had just spoken to them all in the church and explained to them what Riona had done. They were all still in disbelief. The healing would take time.

I knocked on the office door of the abbess.

"Come in."

I entered and walked across the room to her desk. She motioned for me to sit down.

"Deirdre, I have called you here first to thank you for what you did for this monastery. I still am in shock that Sister Riona was behind these murders, but I will pray that God may yet forgive her for her sins."

"Yes, Sister Anna."

"I know that this is not the time for important decisions. You have been through a great deal. The recovery of your grandmother is uncertain. You are exhausted. But you may be wondering if I would allow you to return to the monastery as a nun now that the crisis is over, assuming that is what you want."

"I bear no ill will against you, Sister Anna. I know I disobeyed you. I have no doubt that I deserved to be expelled from this fellowship."

"Indeed you did," she said. "But you may not realize fully why I took the action I did."

"What do you mean?"

"I was very angry at you. You defied me—and not for the first time. I told you that you would have to choose between being a druid and a sister of Brigid. You have tried to walk a path between two worlds that is, in my opinion, impossible to follow. And yet, as you demonstrated on the battlefield this morning, there may be some advantages to being both a Christian and a druid. I am therefore willing to suspend my judgment on the issue. If you want to return to us, you may."

"Thank you, Sister Anna. I am grateful that you would allow me to come back. But as you said, this is a difficult time. May I have a little while to consider it?"

"Yes, of course."

I stood up and bowed, then turned to leave. But I stopped and faced her again.

"Sister Anna, you implied there was some other reason you expelled me from the monastery aside from my disobedience. May I ask what it was?"

"There were two other reasons, actually. The first was so that you might work to solve the mystery of the murders free from the constraints of monastic life. I wanted you to be able to focus all your energies on that task without being a nun. We all suspected that the killer was a druid. I wanted you to have the freedom of a druid as you pursued the killer."

"Yes, I see. That does make sense, Sister Anna."

"I'm so glad you agree."

"But, if I may, what was the other reason?"

Sister Anna stared at me for several moments before speaking.

"I did it to protect you. I knew that a murderer was seeking the lives of the sisters of this monastery. I feared there was nothing I could do to save them, try as I might. The only way I could shield at least one of them was to cast her out, publicly humiliating her so that the whole province would know she was no longer a nun. I wasn't certain it would work, but I hoped it might."

I stood there for a moment, not knowing what to say.

"You mean you did it to keep me safe?"

"Yes."

"But why me?"

"Because you are the most troublesome nun ever to reside inside these walls. If I expelled Sister Darerca or one of the others, the killer might have suspected that I wasn't in earnest. But you—oh, yes—you have been such a well-known thorn in my side that there would be no doubt about my sincerity."

She continued to scowl at me.

"But more than that, Deirdre, let us say that even an abbess can have her favorite."

She returned to her desk and began to work on her abacus. I stood by the door with my mouth half open.

"Sister Anna, I. . . ."

"You are dismissed. I have much work to do."

I bowed again and left, closing the door carefully behind me.

Chapter Twenty-Seven

G randmother, let me do that. You're still not strong
enough."

It was a month after the death of Riona, and my
grandmother and I were in her new home, making dinner for
our guests.

"I can do it, Deirdre. I may not be back to my old self quite
yet, but I can still make sausages."

That morning, we had slaughtered a young sow in the yard.
While my grandmother supervised, I had slit its throat and held
its head while the blood flowed into a large bowl. We would use
most of this later for a tasty pudding. When the pig was dead
and the blood thoroughly drained, I dipped the carcass into a
cauldron of boiling water to remove the hair and hung it by the

feet from the low branch of a tree. I then began butchering the animal. Within minutes, the head had been severed, the carcass split down the middle, and all the organs removed. Nothing went to waste. The bulk of the meat was salted and hung in her smokehouse over a low beech fire to cure for the coming winter, while the loops of intestines were removed and carefully washed to make sausage casings. The head meat would be used for a kind of sweet jelly, the lard rendered to eat with bread or use as a salve, and the skin set aside to fry later with beans.

We were ready to stuff the sausages, and my grandmother insisted that she was perfectly able to blow into one end of the wet intestines to inflate them and make them easier to stuff.

"All right, Grandmother, but don't do too much. Father Ailbe says you have to take it easy."

"Ailbe is a mother hen. I think I know what I can do."

After a minute, she was out of breath and sat down in a chair by the fire.

"Well, maybe I will let you do the rest while I catch my breath for a moment."

My grandmother's new hut was very much like her old one, but had the fragrant smell of fresh wood and thatch. Men from all the surrounding clans had come to build it about a week after the battle, when it was clear that my grandmother would recover. Saoirse's father had brought his grown sons, and they did much of the heavy work themselves. Brion had also sent men from the western clans to labor on the project. The best craftsmen of the tribe had made her new furniture and metal utensils, while a local farmer gave her a fine milk cow. When Grandmother had returned home a couple of weeks later, she complained to me that everything was out of place, but I could tell that she was deeply moved by the generosity of everyone who had helped.

After I had washed at the well, I took most of the organ meat and a small bowl of blood back to the kitchen to make the sausages. There was a brief argument with my grandmother about whether or not to use the spleen for the sausage or cook it separately. I wanted to add it to the rest, but my grandmother liked it fried with onions and nuts. As usual, Grandmother prevailed.

Soon we would fry the sausages and serve them hot, along with leeks and other side dishes. Grandmother had even told me to bring out the jar of Spanish wine that King Dúnlaing had given her.

"They'll be here any minute, Deirdre. Set the table and get out the cups."

"Yes, Grandmother."

There was a knock on the door, and Grandmother insisted on getting up to answer it herself.

"Ailbe, welcome. Dari, come in. Things aren't quite ready yet, but we're working on it. It seems I'm still trying to teach my granddaughter how to cook."

Dari kissed her on the cheek, then came to give me a hand frying the sausages.

"Just like old times, eh?"

"Yes, Dari, though I'm trying to be more patient now."

She smiled and looked up and down at me.

"I like you better in your nun's habit again. Not as flashy as the bardic robe, of course, but still stylish."

There was another knock on the door. My grandmother answered it and welcomed in Cáma and Sinann, the two druids who had been at our interrupted dinner a few weeks earlier.

"It looks like we're all here. Deirdre, are the sausages ready yet?"

"Yes, Grandmother. Everyone can take a seat. Dari, would you pour the wine?"

I set the platter of steaming sausages on the table next to the leeks, relishes, and basket of freshly baked bread with honey butter. My mouth was already watering.

"Ailbe, would you like to say a blessing?" my grandmother asked.

"Gladly, Aoife."

As we bowed our heads, he began.

"Master of the Universe, Creator of us all, grant us your grace over this meal. May it nourish us so that all at this table and those in our hearts may work for peace and healing. Amen."

"Amen," said Dari.

"Amen," said my grandmother and the other druids.

"Amen," I said. "Amen."

Afterword

M ost of what we know about the fascinating world of
the ancient druids comes from descriptions (often
hostile) by Greek and Roman authors, along with a
few stories written by Christians in early Ireland. We know the
druids were priests in much of Celtic Europe and were held in
high esteem by all members of their society. Julius Caesar says
their order originated in Britain and studied up to twenty years
to practice their profession. The Greek philosopher Posidonius,
who traveled in Gaul (modern France) in the early first century
B.C., says they believed in reincarnation, rendered legal judgments, carefully observed the natural world, and performed
sacrifices, occasionally with human victims. He also says they
could stop battles by stepping between armies. Druids could

be either male or female. In fact, of the few individual druids we know from antiquity, most are women.

The myths and legends from early medieval Ireland portray the druids as Merlin-like figures who have much in common with their counterparts in Gaul. But Irish law shows their status sadly declining over the centuries as Christianity spread across the island. Once respected leaders, they were relegated by the church to the fringes of Irish society and reduced to little more than potion-makers and objects of ridicule before they disappeared completely from our view.

For those who would like to learn more about the druids, an excellent book is Miranda Green's *The World of the Druids*, which traces them from their ancient beginnings to modern revival movements. My own *War, Women, and Druids* is a handy translation of almost everything the Greeks and Romans wrote about the religion and life of the pre-Christian Celts, while my *The World of Saint Patrick* gives the Christian point of view in early stories and documents translated from the original Latin and Old Irish, including *The Life of Saint Brigid*, the earliest story we have about any saint from Ireland.

Sacrifice—like *Saint Brigid's Bones* before it—is based as much as possible on what we know from the literature and archaeology of ancient Ireland, but it is a work of fiction.

Many thanks to my friends and colleagues who helped me in shaping the book, especially my wife Alison, my agent Joëlle Delbourgo, and my editor Maia Larson.